Rosemary Friedman's writing career was launched with great success by her first novel *No White Coat*, published in *Best Doctor Stories* alongside Somerset Maugham and A J Cronin. She has gone to write eighteen further novels, including *Proofs of Affection* ('a classic of its kind', *Evening Standard*), which was serialised by the BBC. She has also written two popular children's books, *Aristide* and *Aristide in Paris*, as well as *The Writing Game*, an inspirational memoir for writers and readers.

She has written commissioned screenplays for both film and television in the UK and US, and her play *Home Truths* toured successfully in 1997. In addition, Rosemary has been a judge of literary competitions and a member of a number of distinguished bodies such as the Executive Committee of PEN, BAFTA, the Writers' Guild, the Executive Committee of the Society of Authors, and the Royal Society of Literature. She lives in London.

Rosemary Friedman

Patients of a Saint

HOUSE OF
STRATUS

This edition published in 2001 by House of Stratus, an imprint of Stratus Holdings plc, 24c Old Burlington Street, London, W1X 1RL, UK.

www.houseofstratus.com

Typeset, printed and bound by House of Stratus.

A catalogue record for this book is available from the British Library.

ISBN 0-7551-0114-6

One

"You don't look at all well, Doctor!"

It was this remark repeated many times and with variants ranging from 'You look proper peaky' to 'Reckon you could do with one of your own bottles' that led me, after almost eight years of General Practice to turn firmly in my tracks and take stock of the situation. Who was I and what was I doing? What did I want and where was I going? One more sneaking question: was it a sign of advancing age that led me to ask these semi-philosophical and utterly sober questions? Reluctant to believe that this was in fact the case, I cast round in my mind for one of the customary light-hearted and flippant answers I kept for problems of this sort but to my dismay I found, like Mother Hubbard, that the cupboard was completely bare. It was painfully obvious that the stocktaking, if it was to be done, would have to be carried out on a more serious level.

The first two questions were not difficult to answer. I was an ordinary sort of chap to whom the age of forty no longer seemed like the end of the world but was still sufficiently far away to joke about, I was married to a girl who after a spate of six years was still to me the loveliest thing that ever drew breath, and I had a pair of normal, revolting-wonderful five-year-old children.

What was I doing?

I was responsible for the health of over three thousand seven hundred individuals who were registered with me under the

1

National Health Service and I was attempting (and at times it was no more than an attempt) single-handed, day and night to cope with their needs. On paper it looked ridiculous; in practice it was more so and accounted for the loss of weight, pallor and irritability that the patients, with their usual perspicacity and diagnostic skill, had begun to comment upon.

What did I want?

To my surprise I was no longer able to answer this question. My brain had become a kind of deadly merry-go-round in which how to see more patients in less time, how to cut the corners on my visiting list and how to avoid leaving my bed in the night on the greatest number of occasions seemed to be the monotonously recurring factors. *Peu à peu*, as they say, and virtually without noticing it my professional life had been reduced to a blur. As for where I was going, I no longer knew or cared. I was too tired.

One dreary Monday which as far as work was concerned had started at five in the morning and at nine in the evening had not yet finished, I came out of the surgery and took a long look at myself in the mirror above the morning-room mantelpiece.

I had just stuck out my tongue to its maximum extent and was examining what appeared to be a perfectly normal larynx and at the same time feeling tenderly for any enlarged cervical glands, when Sylvia came in.

"What's the matter with you?" she said.

"I'm overworking!"

The bombshell fell in silence. I replaced my tongue and looked round prepared to justify my shattering statement. Sylvia was writing names in two new, shiny black pairs of Wellington boots with a Biro as if she hadn't heard.

"I said I'm overworking!"

"I heard you."

"Mrs Theobald says I look pale."

No comment.

I pulled at the waistband of my trousers. If I took a deep breath I could just get my hand in between the material and my shirt.

"And I seem to have lost weight lately," I said pathetically.

The pathos fluttered away and disappeared in the lack of response.

"Sylvia," I said, buttoning my jacket and assuming the role of lord and master, "I don't know if I'm imagining things but I appear to be talking to you tonight through an impenetrable curtain. Are you with me or are you not?"

"There's nothing the matter with *me*," she said.

"Well, what's the matter with me?"

"You'd better ask Mrs Theobald."

"Sylvia, I'm tired and if I don't go and give Mrs Calthorpe her injection soon she'll be climbing up the wall. Stop niggling me and tell me what it's all about."

"All right," she said, "I'll tell you. When I married you you were a reasonably good-looking, cheerful, happy, well-adjusted General Practitioner. Look at you now!"

"I just looked," I said.

"I don't mean your tongue. I mean you." She looked me up and down. "Sunken-cheeked, shabby, long-haired, shiny suited, paunchy, harassed, bad-tempered."

"Well!" I said. But she hadn't finished. She stood up, waving a Wellington boot at me threateningly.

"And that's not all! You've a wife and two perfectly adequate children but no one would think so. You've scarcely spoken to us for weeks and as for your sense of humour I think you buried it with old Mr Thomas six months ago."

"The winter's always my busiest time," I said in mitigation.

"Nonsense! It might have been in the old days but now it's exactly the same all year round. If I'd wanted to be married to a miserable, humourless, overworked hack I would have looked for one in the first place."

"It's not even as if we have anything to show for it," I said.

"That's beside the point. And if you'd let me finish…"

"I thought you had."

"Well I haven't. I was about to say that I've been telling you all this for months and you've taken no notice whatsoever, but immediately Mrs Theobald, or whatever her name is, happens to say you look pale you start getting anxious and sticking your tongue out in front of the mirror. I would simply like to remind you, while I seem to have your attention, that you don't happen to be married to the National Health Service, nor to Mrs Theobald."

Sylvia sat down with a thump and left me standing like a naughty schoolboy in the middle of the room.

"Do you remember how we used to laugh?" I said, sitting beside her.

She put down the Wellington and looked at me.

"When people said funny things." She wasn't angry any more.

"Miss Jackson who wanted a sediment because she couldn't sleep."

"And Mrs Gibbs who told you the gland doctor said she had something wrong with her obituary…"

"And when I asked old Miss Parker to show me her teeth and she whipped them out and put them on my desk…" I thought for a moment. "I just don't seem to see the funny side any more."

"You haven't time."

"I know."

"Well, we'll have to do something."

"What?"

"Well, to begin with…" Sylvia said, and then the telephone rang. It was the Reverend Barker ten miles away in Essex with pains in his chest, and I hadn't time to hear how we were to begin.

With the passing of years, my practice had gradually become more widespread. It had started off neatly and conveniently in a rough circle whose radius extended a mile or two only from my surgery which was attached to the house. As time went by and my patients either outgrew their houses or for some reason or other decided to move, they would ask me, having become accustomed to my ways, whether I would continue to look after them in the district to which they were going. If it was not an unreasonable distance I usually said yes. Those who cared enough about me to ask me to remain their family doctor were usually those people to whom over the years I had become quite attached – in the beginning I was most flattered that they preferred my attentions rather than welcoming a change of medical practitioner. Now, however, things had developed so rapidly that the extent of my practice could no longer be clearly defined and, as in the case of the Reverend Barker, I found myself, usually at the most inconvenient moments, doing visits ten and even fifteen miles away.

The Reverend Barker was, as he put it, 'living on tick'; only it wasn't a washing-machine or a television he was borrowing, but his life. When I first started in practice he had a small living in the district. He had a wife and five children, but I rarely saw them, although they were on my list, because they were both considerate and healthy. One hot Saturday afternoon about three years earlier, little Christine Barker had knocked on our door with a polite message from her mother that they hated to bother me but her father had been mowing the lawn when suddenly he had a severe pain in his chest, felt ill and was now lying on the sofa. Would it be too much trouble…? But already my geiger counter was ticking furiously. "I shan't be long," I remember saying to Sylvia. "Reverend Barker's had a coronary." It wasn't a spot diagnosis without having seen the patient; nor yet a shot, blindly, in the dark. Neither could it in any sense be called intuition. It was just that after a certain number of years in General Practice events began to form a pattern, the higgledy-piggledy train of apparently unconnected happenings to take shape. It wasn't just the polite little picture Christine Barker had painted; it was the whole set-up I was taking into account and it was one I had seen, unfortunately, too many times. A hitherto healthy male, age between forty and fifty, harassed and overworked, sudden physical exertion, severe pain in the chest region… I could have been wrong but I didn't think I would be. I wasn't. A few weeks later, when the Reverend was convalescing and I was paying him a routine visit, he said to me:

"Let us discuss things, Doctor."

He was sitting up in bed and I was putting away my sphygmomanometer.

"Certainly," I said. "What things?"

"The prognosis. I did not get to meet my Maker this time. I should like to know, in your opinion, how long it will be before I have the pleasure of doing so."

He betrayed no more emotion than if he were discussing an invitation to the Church Bazaar.

"You mustn't worry about things like that," I said. "You'll be fine in a few weeks. Of course you'll have to take things more easily…"

"I'm not in the slightest bit worried," he said, "you must know that. It's simply that I have to make plans. I have six dependants. If you would entrust me with them I would prefer to have facts rather than placation. I must make my arrangements and I have seen enough of my parishioners with this complaint to know that I may have to leave this world a little sooner than I anticipated."

"I wish more of my patients had your courage, Reverend," I said.

He looked surprised. "It's not courage," he said, "it's faith and its available to all."

Since the Reverend Barker was one of the few patients who were able to look it in the face with equanimity, I decided it would be best to tell him the truth. His coronary thrombosis had been a severe one and it was likely that, in the not too distant future, he would have another. I advised him to cut down on his activities and painted the prognosis, which was not very bright, as lightly as I could.

It was like advising a fish to stop swimming. The Reverend Barker was quite incapable of cutting down on his activities; if anything, he increased his efforts to safeguard the future of his family. When he was offered, a year or so later, a large and important living in Essex, he had no hesitation in accepting it. When he outlined the duties it brought with it in addition to the extra salary, I said:

"You know it will probably kill you." But he replied:

"It is a call from God."

And now it seemed that his coronary circulation had let him down again; I was surprised that it hadn't happened before.

It took me about twenty minutes to get to the Barkers' house in Essex, but there was no panic when I arrived. The house was larger than the one they had had previously but there were no more concessions to comfort. The Reverend Barker never grumbled, nor complained, nor even mentioned it to me but I knew that there simply wasn't the money, for all his hard work, for there to be.

Mrs Barker told me that her husband had gone to bed early complaining of fatigue. Just before she rang me, he had had an attack of pain similar to his previous one.

She led the way up the uncarpeted stairs to the large bedroom which said more volubly than any words that here there was not a spare penny for anything other than the barest essentials of existence.

The Reverend Barker was too ill to talk. I did what was necessary then went downstairs with his wife.

"Another attack?" she said.

"I'm afraid it is."

"Will he be all right?"

"I think he will this time," I said. "Although it's difficult to be absolutely sure."

I told her to ring me if she was worried during the night, and that if I hadn't heard from her before I would see her husband again in the morning.

"I'm sorry," I said at the door by way of comfort.

Mrs Barker smiled. "The Lord will provide," she said. And as I went down the garden path, stumbling, for there was no light, I realised that she was comforting me.

I dealt with Mrs Calthorpe on my way back, and with two other visits which had come in during the evening Surgery.

When I got home Sylvia was in bed, reading. While I undressed I told her about the Reverend Barker. She always took a personal interest in the patients, and I liked to keep her up to date so that when I was out she could deal with the telephone calls and assess, in the light of her knowledge, their urgency.

"Is he still so complacent about it all?" Sylvia asked.

"About what?"

"Dying."

"He was too ill. His wife was, though."

"Aren't they lucky. It gives me the heeby-jeebies."

"Perhaps you should go to church more often."

"When do you suggest? Sunday mornings are getting almost as busy as Mondays. Which brings me to what we were talking about earlier on."

I yawned and got into bed, checking up that my torch and jersey, in case of night calls, were *in situ.*

"Yes. I'm curious to hear what plans you have buzzing round in that pretty little head of yours."

I lay back on the pillow, luxuriating.

"Well, to begin with – " Sylvia said. There was a knocking, like a persistent mouse, at the door.

"Yes?"

The handle jiggled a few times, then the door opened slowly. A small head appeared, its hair sticking up in short, dark spikes, its face sleep-rumpled.

"Daddy?"

"Well?"

He padded over to the bed, uncertain of his welcome.

"Penny's firsty!"

"So?"

He looked surprised. "She wants a grink."

It was a curious thing about the twins. They ran errands for each other like Ike and Mike. If Penny was thirsty Peter was the courier. If Peter discovered a hole in his sheet, Penny would bear the terrible news. They were a sort of mutual-protection society and I suppose they believed that it added weight to their requests if they were relayed by the other half of the partnership.

I dealt with Penny's thirst which was, as usual, secondary to the desire for a companionable chat in the still hours of the long night, and resumed contact with my pillow.

"Now – " Sylvia said. But she got no further. This time it was the telephone.

"I suppose I shall have to go back to Essex," I said, feeling not the least like it and presuming it was Mrs Barker to say that her husband was worse.

It wasn't; it was Faraday, my friend, colleague and best man at my wedding. He was babbling like an idiot.

Sylvia, curious as usual, leaned over my shoulder.

"What's he talking about?"

"Haven't a clue. He's either in a state of acute mania or he's drunk. I think he said something about getting married."

"But that's wonderful!" Sylvia said. We had been trying to get Faraday married for years.

But it wasn't Faraday who was getting married at all. When he calmed down a little he told me that he had just heard that his Chief, at the hospital, an elderly widower, was shortly to marry an American heiress and was sailing away with her round the world. Faraday was his Senior Registrar and had been jogging along with fading hopes of ever getting a Consultantship for years. There was no guarantee now that he would get the post but the odds were pretty good. Faraday, near-genius, and slogger supreme, was beside himself with joy.

I wished him luck and Sylvia at my elbow shouted her wishes down the phone.

"You weren't asleep?" Faraday remembered to say when his excitement had died down.

"No. Not asleep."

"OK," he said. "I'll keep you posted."

"Do that," I said. "Let me know the minute you hear anything."

"The very minute!"

I was about to say goodbye but he'd already hung up.

"Exciting," I said. "I hope he gets it."

"So do I." Sylvia laid down. "What was I saying?"

"I can't remember. I don't think I can stay awake much longer."

"Nor me."

"Shall we leave it till the morning?"

"Let's."

"Goodnight, Sweetie," I said.

"Goodnight."

Two

But the morning, as we might have known had we considered it, saw us caught up in our customary medical and domestic ballet which left no time at all for conversation. I say ballet. There was no muted settling and last-minute coughs before curtain-up; no sweet, plinking tuning of violins; no breathless, soul-squeezing anticipatory excitement. Like a nightmare, it just began, with a bang, at seven o'clock and with everything happening.

Penny fell into the room to announce that it was a quarter past eleven and that they'd be late for school; at the same time the telephone rang with the news that Mrs Clamp was in labour, and the doorbell pealed twice and urgently because the postman couldn't get the parcel of X-ray films through the letter-box. I got up to deal with the postman and Mrs Clamp, and Sylvia to rouse from her bed of roses our current *au pair*, a young lady from Switzerland who seemed never to have her fill of sleep, and whose job it was, ostensibly, to cope with these early morning crises – apart, of course, from Mrs Clamp.

After this brusque beginning I caught only brief glimpses of Sylvia throughout the day. While I was with Mrs Clamp she gave the children breakfast; while I came back for a quick cup of coffee she took the children to school; at lunch-time Mrs Clamp gave birth; I ate my dried-up Lancashire hot-pot at four while Sylvia was taking the twins to have their hair cut; I was

11

back in the surgery while she was putting them to bed; while she had dinner Mrs Clamp had a secondary haemorrhage.

At eleven o'clock we met in the bedroom.

"How do you do?" I said.

"Pleased to meet you." Sylvia was sewing a button on my shirt.

"This can't go on."

"Agreed."

"We must do something."

"I have!" She cut the cotton and admired her handiwork.

"How do you mean?"

"We're going away for the weekend."

"Impossible! Where to?"

"Limmering. Why?"

"The children."

"I've spoken to your mother. She'll have them."

"The patients."

"I met Dr Miller in the High Street. She doesn't mind doing a weekend for you."

"You shouldn't have asked her."

"Well, I did. Any more objections?"

"I've made appointments for Saturday."

"Well, you can unmake them."

"Huh!" I said cynically.

"Tell me what they are."

"Well, I'm assisting Heatherington with Mrs Bridgewater. She's having her veins stripped."

"Heatherington was stripping veins before you were born. Next?"

"An insurance examination for the Mutual at five-thirty."

"He can come next Saturday."

"Baby Neville-Browne's third polio. I promised to go up to the Priory," I said weakly.

"Well, that's fine!" Sylvia got into bed. "We leave after lunch on Friday."

12

"What about the telephone?" I said triumphantly from my last ditch. "Annalies can't even hear it, let alone answer it adequately."

"Your mother is coming to stay here," Sylvia said. "She was quite pleased. It's cold at Frinton."

So that was how we came, one freezing Saturday afternoon in February, to be sitting as close as we could get, which wasn't very, to a blazing log fire in the lounge of the Mulberry Hotel at Limmering.

Until the last minute I hadn't actually believed that we should get away. It was not only that I was so busy but that mentally I had got so deep into a rut that I felt both incapable of, and loath to pull myself out of it. If it hadn't been for Sylvia's helping hand I should never have been able to make the effort at all. I suppose that's why they call them helpmeets and, to mix my metaphors, when mine had her dander up she could really dig her heels in.

It was Sylvia who packed; Sylvia who told the patients gently but firmly on the telephone I would not be available until Monday but that they could consult Dr Miller if they wished; Sylvia who wrote out for my mother a list of instructions about a yard long concerning the welfare of the twins and the practice (this she need not have bothered with because my mother cared not a jot for rules or regulations and made up her own as she went along); Sylvia who finally and categorically hugged the children on Friday after lunch and shepherded me with my dragging feet into the car.

Physically I was in the car, making for the Great West Road. Mentally I was still at home.

"I hope Mother remembers to stick a notice on the door if she goes out."

"She will."

"I forgot to leave Mr Adams' prescription."

"Dr Miller will give it to him."

"She won't know what it is."

13

"She can come in and look up his notes."

"Oh! Yes!" The cynicism was due to the fact that it was years since I had had time to search for everybody's medical record as they came in and make notes about them. Any memoranda I made were in my head. Perhaps that accounted for the peculiar feeling I had had for the past few months that it was going to burst at any moment.

At Staines Sylvia said: "Look, you might as well relax. We're not turning back now so you just forget about the patients. We're on holiday and I'm sure it will ultimately be for their own good. You'll come back a new man."

There was something in what she said. I smiled, which is more difficult than it sounds when your face is permanently tensed up and everything seems to be a matter of life and death, eased my foot from the accelerator, dropping down to sixty, and put my arm round Sylvia.

"Whoops!" Sylvia said as we scraped past a petrol lorry, "there's no need to go from one extreme to the other."

But I did. We were on holiday. We sang. We stopped for tea at a pull-up for car men. We listened to Radio Luxembourg. We didn't care. By the time we arrived at Limmering it was pouring with rain and the Mulberry Hotel looked as forbidding and deserted as seaside hotels always do in the winter. We still didn't care.

In the hall, which was warm but ghostly quiet, a lady in a skirt and jumper said, "thirty - faive - and - six - a - day - special - winter - rates - and - no - cooked - breakfasts - served - in - the - bedrooms." She asked our names and Sylvia opened her mouth to say "Doctor and Mrs…" when I trod, unfortunately more firmly than I had intended, on her toe.

Sylvia said "Ouch", and the lady in the skirt and jumper snapped her mouth shut disapprovingly, looking at each of us in turn with suspicion, and I said, "*Mr* and Mrs…" looking her fairly and squarely in the eye and daring her to say we don't have 'that sort of thing here'.

Having completed the formalities to her satisfaction the lady said "Number naine" and, taking a key from the hook behind her, came out from behind her desk and indicated with a sniff that we were to follow her.

We passed the glass doors of the lounge on the way to the stairs and, glancing in, I was glad that at the risk of maiming Sylvia I had managed to avoid letting on that I was a doctor. There were six people in the room; one man and five women. At a quick guess I estimated the combined ages to be some four hundred years, and there was little doubt that between them they would be able to produce enough operations and illnesses to while away an entire weekend. In such a milieu a doctor was fair game. I was not willing if they were.

The first thing I did in our neat but freezing bedroom in which the lady in the skirt and jumper had uncertainly left us alone with the warning that dinner, off-season, was at six-thirty, was to disconnect the telephone; the second was to put a shilling in the meter and switch on the electric fire; the third was to put my arms round Sylvia who was huddling into her coat.

I kissed her passionately then said, looking over her shoulder, "Blast!"

"What's the matter?"

"We've got single beds."

"I know."

"Why didn't you say something then while our friend was here?"

"I didn't like to make an issue out of it. She's highly suspicious as it is."

"Perhaps you're right. We don't want to create a furore. We shall just have to manage."

"How do you mean, manage?"

"In one."

Sylvia looked. "There seem to be two to me."

"We'd be cold. Besides we're on our second honeymoon."

15

"What about that weekend in Paris after the twins were born?"

"Third then."

"And the week at Turnberry after my appendix?"

"Fourth then. Anyway who's counting?"

"Not me," Sylvia said, stroking my hair.

"Nor me." I held her close.

At dinner-time we presented ourselves in the dining-room on the stroke of six-thirty and even then we appeared to be late.

The residents were already seated, their bottles of Mist. Mag. Trisil and vitamin capsules in front of them, at their tables for one, when we appeared to take our seats. Spoons were halted midway from plates to mouths, arthritic fingers paused in attempts to break crusty rolls, mulligatawny soup was momentarily forgotten.

I remembered an old trick from my schooldays. It was called 'staring out'. When we were seated at our centre table, like the cabaret act, in full view of everyone, I chose the nearest pair of eyes. They belonged to a stout lady in a mothy-looking fur. I waited until she had priced Sylvia, hair, dress, handbag, brooch and shoes, and swivelled her attention to me. She got no further than the top of my head when I fixed my eyes on hers, riveted them there, and did not blink. Mesmer could not have done better. Surprised, as if in some indecent act, the stout party reddened to the navy-blue roots of her ginger hair and addressed her roll and butter. I noticed the slimming tablets on her table and made a bet with myself that she would not only work her way solidly through the menu but would have second helpings of everything. Having dealt with this lady, who was the nearest, I worked my way methodically round the room, and only when I had routed the entire army did I turn my attention to my soup.

This, however, was only the first round.

After dinner we repaired to the lounge, a compulsory move if we wanted coffee, which we did, and sat as near as we were able to the fire. Since the five ladies and the one gentleman had got there first and I suppose by virtue of their long tenure had prior claims, we were in actual fact nearer to the French windows than the hearth. We weren't too worried; both of us exhausted, we didn't intend staying long and, to do the residents justice they did half-heartedly shuffle their chairs as if they were making room when we came in. I didn't believe though that any one of them actually budged half an inch.

The coffee was surprisingly good. Sylvia was pouring a second cup for both of us when a voice said, loudly and clearly, "Was it raining in London?" and after a moment or two of silence I realised they were talking to us.

A fierce-looking battle-axe in mauve, wearing pince-nez and with a walking stick by her chair, waited for an answer. So did the other five. A tiny old lady fiddled with the battery on her hearing-aid.

"What was that?" she piped.

The lady in mauve leaned towards her.

"I asked them if it was raining in London," she boomed, and then she turned to us.

"Miss Trapp needs a new battery," she said.

I nodded understandingly and Sylvia smiled.

"Was it?" the mauve lady said.

We drank our coffee while the clock ticked, the fire popped and speculation rose silently.

"Perhaps you'd like a peppermint cream with your coffee?" The box was extended by a veined hand shaking with the rapid tremor of Parkinsonism.

"I won't. Thank you so much."

"Perhaps your..." there was the barest moment of hesitation, "...wife would like one?"

Sylvia out of the kindness of her heart took one. I knew she hated peppermint. I signalled to her to hurry, knowing that if we did not remove ourselves we should be entrenched until cocoa-time. It was an old game they were playing and they were skilled players. Already with one question and a peppermint they had

17

established (a) that we came from London and (b) – because we had not become discomfited at the artless remark – that we were in fact man and wife. If we stayed very much longer I guaranteed that before I knew it they would have my income out of me and how often I changed my socks; I couldn't hope to beat them at their own game and anyway I had no desire to.

I whispered to Sylvia the suggestion that we should get our coats and go for a blow before bed and we made a move. At the bottom of the stairs I realised that I had left my newspaper in the lounge.

"Carry on," I said to Sylvia, "I'd better retrieve it."

Their heads were together and they didn't see me come in.

"What was that?" Miss Trapp was saying.

"The Colonel said they must be on their honeymoon!" the lady with Parkinson's enunciated as clearly as she could.

I picked up my newspaper.

"Fourth!" I said cheerfully. They looked at me in horror. "Or possibly fifth. One loses count." I leered a lecherous leer which I hoped made me look like Casanova and left them to this tit-bit.

Later in my narrow bed without the customary comfort of Sylvia's back, I tossed and turned listening to the distant banging of the sea and waiting, half-expectantly as I did at home, for the telephone to ring. I knew I was on holiday but was unable to unwind; my motor had been coiled too tightly. After about half an hour I gave up tossing and turning and started moaning and groaning in the selfish hope that Sylvia would hear. I hadn't the courage to wake her in cold blood. The response was immediate. It was obvious she hadn't been able to sleep either.

She didn't say anything but switched on the lamp and hopped out of bed. I watched curiously as she took something from her make-up case. She came back to me holding it in the palm of her hand.

"Take this," she commanded.

I sat up. "What is it?"

"A seconal."

"Where did you get it?"

"From your dispensary. I knew you wouldn't be able to relax just like that."

"I've never taken a sleeping-pill in my life."

Sylvia picked up the glass of water by the bed.

"Well, you're going to now."

And I did. And twelve oblivious, uninterrupted hours later I woke to find the Limmering sun flooding through the windows. I was about to say to Sylvia I'll have my bath while you listen for the telephone, when I suddenly realised where I was and that if Jimmy Jones was 'smothered' in a rash or Mr Matthews had another of his 'turns' in the night it was no concern of mine. I hoped that Phoebe Miller was coping and Mother making not too much of a hash of the telephone messages, chipping in with her own advice as she always did, but it was as much as I could do to make myself care. Home and the practice were fading away into the unreal middle-distances of my mind. I was happy, a free man, on holiday. I bounced out of bed.

Stimulated by my night's sleep and the glorious prospect of a sunny morning by the sea I saw my fellow inmates through eyes less jaundiced than I had the night before. I felt all things to all men.

"Good morning!" I called to the lady of the slimming tablets battling her stout way against the wind along the sea-front. "Good morning!" I boomed into Miss Trapp's hearing-aid as we passed her huddled into the corner seat of a municipal shelter.

"Good morning, Colonel," I said heartily to the old man, striding, *Times* beneath his arm, towards the harbour. It was good to be alive.

After lunch we decided that we had had enough fresh air and the best of the day; the sun had disappeared and there was an icy wind blowing in from the sea.

Quite content and with faces tingling still from the air, we settled in the lounge for coffee. Already we felt like members of the family, and they had all actually moved their chairs an inch or two to make room for us near the fire.

The fat lady and the one with the stick had settled to a cosy appraisal of their various operations to which I listened with amusement. My eyes met Sylvia's and I knew she was thinking, as I was, how sensible it had been of me to conceal my identity. There was no reason, I thought, for them to imagine for a moment that I was a doctor.

But I had reckoned without Miss Trapp.

One moment she was sitting in her chair fiddling with her battery and trying to hear the more relevant details of the conversation going on next to her, and the next she was lying in a small, crumpled heap on the floor.

Sylvia said: "Sweetie!"

The fat lady clutched her bosom dramatically and the Colonel said:

"Fetch the MO."

Unfortunately I hadn't time to see their reactions as I straightened poor little Miss Trapp out and tried to assess what had happened to her. I heard the babbling of voices behind me from which I was able to distinguish the words "…brandy" (the Colonel), "…eau-de-Cologne" (the lady with the stick), "…water" (the manageress who had come in to see what all the noise was about) and Sylvia explaining to them that I was a doctor.

Miss Trapp appeared to have had a slight stroke. With the agreement of all and sundry I sent for the ambulance which took her to the nearest hospital, telephoned her sister in Brighton, and assured the manageress that there was every chance that she would be fit enough in a few weeks to resume her residence.

When I got back to the lounge there was a decided atmosphere.

"Poor Miss Trapp," was the opening gambit.

Then, "We had no idea..." The fat lady was looking at me with admiration and I was sure a long list of questions concerning her weight.

"A touch of the old arthritis..." the Colonel began but was interrupted by the lady with the stick.

"What sort of a doctor are you...?" She leaned towards me eagerly and I felt myself cornered.

I looked appealingly at my helpmate.

"My husband is a specialist," she said, and I looked at her with horror, thinking she must have gone mad, "in venereal disease!"

There was a shocked silence and they all seemed to shrink away.

The fat lady was the first to recover.

"I wonder if Miss Trapp is well enough for grapes," she said primly, and I felt myself relegated to purdah.

Up in the bedroom to which we escaped we rolled on the beds with laughter.

"What an inspiration!" I said to Sylvia. "However did you think of it?"

But Sylvia was shaking, tears streaming down her face with her mascara. "Oh dear," she sobbed, "the expressions on their faces."

During our morning walk we had had a long discussion about how to ease my lot as far as the practice was concerned and had come to the following conclusions:

(a)   I was to get an assistant to share the work with me,

(b)   We were to consider moving so that we should not have the strain of 'living over the shop' where the patients knew I was available and vulnerable night and day.

Simple decisions both, yet ones we had needed the perspective, lent by distance, to make.

We prepared to go home, looking forward to putting our resolutions into practice.

21

Saturday night and Sunday morning passed slowly. Working like an automaton as I had been, I hadn't realised that there were so many hours in the day. By Sunday afternoon they appeared to be crawling by and I was getting quite itchy to be back at work.

Since Sylvia's bombshell on Saturday afternoon we had been treated by all at the Mulberry with polite restraint. The only acceptable topic of conversation appeared by common consent to be Miss Trapp, whose condition we heard was improving. Only the Colonel had been giving me, throughout Sunday, queer, sidelong glances. I discovered the reason for these just as we were about to leave.

I was in the hall with our bags, when he detached himself from his lady friends in the lounge and drew me to one side. He glanced about him to see if anyone was looking.

"Herrumph!" he said. Then, "Doctor?" conspiratorially.

I said "Yes?" a little impatiently; Sylvia was waiting in the car.

"Yer know y'said you're a specialist in the old Clap!" he said. "I was wonderin' whether I might consult you about m'self!"

The poor old boy looked crestfallen when, having finally assembled his courage to broach the subject, I had to set fire to his illusions about me. I gave him the address of a colleague of mine who would be able to help him, and we drove away from Limmering.

"Who would think it of the old boy?" Sylvia said as we made for the open road.

"You never can tell," I said wisely.

"At least we've given them something to talk about," Sylvia said. "We shall probably last for the best part of the week."

I laughed.

Sylvia said: "Don't laugh. It's rather sad to think of them all sitting there year after year, discussing their complaints until they get carted off like Miss Trapp."

I put my foot on the accelerator and thought of the log fire, the cups of coffee and the medicine bottles at the Mulberry. The same little play, enacted with the same cast, day after day.

"Sometimes you must laugh," I said, "when the alternative is to cry."

Three

I had given my key to Mother, and Sylvia had lent hers to Doctor Miller; since Annalies had the third one I had to ring the bell when we arrived home on Sunday night.

We heard the bell ring but there was no reply.

"Perhaps Mother has the children in the bath," Sylvia said.

I rang again. "I hope everything's all right."

After a few moments the door was opened; but not by Mother.

A blonde in skin-tight, scarlet trousers, black sweater and bare feet stood in the doorway smiling at us through horn-rimmed spectacles perched on a retroussé, freckled nose.

"Hy!" She raised an arm in greeting and a cascade of bangles jangled to rest at her elbow. "I'm Caroline. C'mon in."

I stared at her. It couldn't be.

"You're not...?" I began.

"Sure am," she said, "little Cousin Caroline from the States grewed up. Hy'a Doc." She threw her arms round my neck and it was like having Brigitte Bardot and Marilyn Monroe in your arms all at once (or at least I imagine so). Since I was holding a suitcase in each hand I was powerless to detach her. I could feel Sylvia bristling and looked across at her to say something but my mouth was full of blonde hair.

When she did finally release me and we went inside I said:

"Where's Mother?" There was no sign of the children.

Caroline said: "Anty had to go on back to Frinton. Her neighbour called she had a burst pipe."

"And the children?" Sylvia said anxiously.

"The kids are fine. They're in back fixing supper from the ice-box."

We made a dive for the kitchen, expecting to see our pair of angels in their Clydella dressing-gowns sitting at the table with their bedtime cereal. At the doorway we stopped and stared. Penny, looking more fifteen than five, was dressed in pale-pink, frilly, baby-doll pyjamas; she had bare feet, her hair piled on top of her head and finished with a huge pink bow, and she was sitting on the draining-board, her legs swinging, gnawing at a leg of chicken.

"Hy!" she said, raising her eyes for a moment, then went back to her bone.

All we could see of Peter was his behind across which rode a success of cowboys on bucking broncos; the rest of him was in the fridge.

Caroline said: "Pete. Your Mom and Pop are here." When he turned round we saw that the broncos were bucking over his chest as well. There was jam on his face and he was clutching a bowl of trifle.

"Hy," he said and, padding on his bare feet over to the drawer, took out a spoon.

The telephone rang. Mother's voice, sounding as if she was in Finland rather than in Frinton, crackled over the line.

"I'm terribly sorry, darling," she said, "but I had to come back; the house is practically flooded. It was a good thing Mrs Hill noticed it. I hope everything's all right and that Caroline is coping. The children adore her. I left you some cold chicken and trifle in the fridge, so you won't have to worry about supper."

I looked at Penny who had started on her second chicken leg.

"Everything's fine, Mother," I said. "Thank you for everything. Is there anything I can do for you?"

"Well, it's a bit wet here," Mother said, "but I'll soon have it shipshape. Must run, darling, the plumber wants something. Just rang to see if you were back. And darling..."

"Yes?"

"Can't you do something about Mrs Porter? She has four under five and another on the way; she came round on Saturday about her milk certificate. She looks worn out, poor soul."

"It's not my fault."

"I know, dear. I think you should have a word with her husband. It's scandalous."

"She hasn't got one," I said.

"Hasn't got what?"

"A husband." There was a hush and I could imagine Mother trying to work that one out.

"Well, see what you can do," she said finally and hung up. I wasn't sure what she meant.

Sylvia carted the children off to bed although they protested that Cousin Caroline had promised they could watch 'Murder down the Line' at nine o'clock, and I had a look at my message pad by the telephone. Saturday's messages in Mother's exemplary copperplate seemed quite straightforward. The page headed Sunday was closely filled with tiny, almost illegible writing from which I could just decipher such words as 'allergy', 'coronary heart disease' and 'penicillin'.

I looked at Caroline. She took the message pad from me and pushed her spectacles higher up her nose.

"The small Tanner kid complained of inability to breathe through his nose," she read as though it were a deposition. "On being questioned the mother admitted he had had the condition for some years and that it was worse in the early spring and summer. There is a family history of asthma and eczema so I presoomed it was not unlikely he was suffering from an allergic rhinitis. I told her you would no doubt make arrangements for the child to be seen by an Allergist who would skin-test him and..."

"Nose drops," I said, writing on my prescription pad. "Next."

Caroline frowned. "Mr Stack," she said; "pains in the chest suggestive of coronary heart disease…"

"Coronary foot disease!" I said. "He doesn't want to go back to work tomorrow. Did you ring Dr Miller?"

"Sure!" Caroline looked hurt.

"OK. Carry on."

"Mrs Rudd, a boil on her arm; said it could wait until tomorrow but I told her it might be dangerous to neglect it and that she should call Dr Miller to give her a shot."

"Phoebe will be thrilled."

"I guess that was all except for a query."

"What was that?"

"Somebody called to see if you accepted new patients. I said I guessed so but wasn't sure about the fees."

I sighed. "Caroline," I said. "Haven't you heard of the National Health Service?"

"Guess not," she said, and I presumed that was two more prospective patients down the drain.

Annalies being out, we had supper, what Penny had left of the chicken and Peter of the trifle, in the kitchen.

Caroline sprawled her bare feet under the table, her elbows on top of it, and ate her chicken like Henry the Eighth.

"What are you over here for, Caroline?" I asked.

"Sex," she said, chewing at her wing.

I thought perhaps it was something to do with her accent.

"What was that?"

"Sex."

"That's what I thought you said. Isn't it rather a long way to come? I mean couldn't you have got fixed up in the States?"

"Oh it's not for me personally," she said, picking delicately at the bone. "I'm a Sociology student (she said stoodent) and I'm doing a survey on 'The sexual behaviour of the teenager in the Western world'. They've given me England."

"That's nice of them."

"How long are you here for?" Sylvia said.

"Six months."

"Where are you staying?" I asked.

"Anty offered to put me up…" I wondered if my mother who I was sure had never uttered the word in her life, and subscribed to the birds and bees theory, knew why Caroline was in England.

But Caroline was saying "…of course it's terrible cute down at Frinton but rather depopulated. I don't think they go in for teenagers."

"Of course not," I said. "Frinton's where people retire to. Look," I said and felt Caroline's shoe beneath the table dig sharply into my shin, "why don't you stay here with us? We've plenty of room and in thirty minutes you're in the West End which is thick with teenagers." And then I realised that Caroline wasn't wearing shoes and that it was Sylvia who had kicked me. But it was too late.

Caroline's arms were round my neck. "You're a darling!" she said. And then to Sylvia: "Isn't he just a hunk of blueberry-pie?"

"Listen, you hunk of blueberry-pie," Sylvia said to me later that evening while we were waiting for Caroline to finish in the bathroom. "Having done the damage, you'd better watch yourself with that sexy flesh-pot of a cousin of yours."

"She's only *studying* it," I said. "In teenagers."

"I wouldn't be so sure," Sylvia said, "judging by the arms-round-your neck every five minutes routine. And anyway I thought you told me your cousin Caroline in New York was an ugly monkey with pigtails?"

"So she was last time I saw her."

"When was that?"

I thought. "Must be ten years."

"And another thing," Sylvia said. "I don't think she's a good influence on the children."

"Why's that?"

"She's given Penny a miniature make-up outfit and taught her how to spit into the mascara, and Peter asked me what 'alimony' meant."

"Don't worry, Sweetie," I said. "She'll settle down and if she doesn't we can always pass her on to somebody else. She is my first cousin all said and done; one has to be hospitable. And at least we shall have a sitter when Annalies goes."

I thanked Phoebe Miller for coping with my patients while I had been away. As usual she said exactly what she thought:

"If your wife hadn't told me you were practically fading away from exhaustion I would never have done it. I've more than enough to do with m'own practice this time of the year; added to which Clarence has had the most fearful bout of gastro-enteritis; nearly lost him."

I murmured sympathetically. Clarence was her dog.

"Was up till midnight on Saturday," she carried on, "quite unnecessary – don't know why they can't use their common sense a bit instead of running to the telephone every time they sneeze. Milksops! That's what we're breeding now; milksops. When I started in practice they'd need to be practically dying before they'd send for the doctor."

"They had to consider his fee, then," I said. Phoebe Miller had never taken kindly to the Health Service.

"Fee fiddlesticks! Had more self-respect and respect for the doctor." We had been standing on the pavement. She got into her car and started the engine. I saw her mouthing something at me but since the window was closed couldn't hear a word. She wound it down.

"I said you should get an assistant!"

"I'm going to," I said.

"Good. I don't want to do any more of your weekends. I've enough of m'own troubles."

She drove off with three of her dogs gazing mournfully at me from the back window.

There was something in what she said but only something. Old-style practitioners such as Phoebe Miller had found it difficult to adapt themselves to the rough and tumble of the New Order. And rough and tumble it certainly was. While the National Health Service was on the whole, from both the patients' and the doctors' point of view, an excellent scheme, it was subject to certain abuses. The chief of these was the attitude of some members of the general public of 'Well, we're payin', aren't we?' They were of course paying but GPs, even under the terms of the Health Service Act, remained human and they hadn't increased the number of hours in the day. Perhaps the worst offenders were the mothers of young children who seemed quite to have lost their powers of judgement and were passing on their irresponsible attitude to the next generation. A child had only to come home from school at teatime with a headache or sore throat for its mother to be on the telephone demanding an immediate visit. From the mother's point of view and from my own this was, in most cases, a waste of time. At this early stage few physical signs would be apparent and a visit the following morning when whatever the child was cooking up became obvious was nearly always necessary. Had the mother merely put the child to bed when it came home from school, watched it and called in the morning if it seemed necessary, the child would be none the worse and the doctor most likely a great deal better for being saved one, of very many unnecessary calls.

"I thought if we caught it early we could nip it in the bud," was a common excuse for these premature consultations. It was, of course, an excellent attitude and one we liked to encourage in cases of suspected malignant growths or blood disorders; but we still could not go round pumping antibiotics into every 'off-colour' schoolchild with a temperature before it was possible to make a diagnosis. Bed, rest and a mother's care were in many cases far more beneficial than a few 'tuts-tuts' and a bottle of linctus from us.

My mother belongs to the old, pre-Health Service school.

On the Sunday night of our return from Limmering we had found by Penny's bed a jug, the syrupy-looking contents of which took me, with no nostalgia, back to my childhood.

"Penny had a cough," Peter explained, "so Granny gave it to her with a teaspoon."

"What is it?" It smelled pleasant enough.

"Glytherine, honey and lemon."

Of course; it always had been for coughs, and cinnamon in milk for colds. And it was not as stupid as it seemed.

Cough mixtures were one of the biggest myths of our day and age and 99 per cent of them were useless and would have been equally effective poured down the sink. When someone had a cough the area that was inflamed and caused the cough was the lining of the bronchi which branched from the trachea in the top portion of the chest. The strongest cough medicine in the world, however frequently swallowed, was not able, since it was not anatomically possible, to get anywhere near this region on its way to the stomach. The only tickly portion it did leave was the back of the throat which could be equally well soothed by any warm or syrupy household beverage – such as the rather complicated one my mother had administered to Penny. The only cough mixtures which were of any real value whatsoever were the sedative ones to be taken at night. These depressed the cough centres in the brain and alleviated the spasm. The same effect would have been achieved by the administration of the sedative without the linctus. These facts were something that the public, brainwashed by the advertisers of patent medicines, were quite unwilling to accept, and I had long ago, in company with most of my colleagues, who had after all to eat, and support their families, given up trying.

If the patients demanded a 'cough bottle', they got it. If it wasn't strong enough or nasty enough to be effective they got a stronger and nastier one. By the time they had swallowed the lot the cough was usually better. They refused to believe that the only people to benefit from the contents of the bottle were the drug firms. The ruling was 'the worse the cough the darker the bottle'. It smacked of faith-healing but there it was. There was no more to be said.

On the night of our return from our blissful weekend in Limmering we had been asleep for about two hours when the telephone rang. From the black depths of my dreams I eventually found the receiver and answered it. The conversation went like this:

"Hallo."

"Hallo. Is that you, Doctor?"

"Yes."

"This is Mr Butterworth. I'm sorry to trouble you at this time of night but I was wondering whether you could come round."

"What's the trouble?"

"It's Mrs Butterworth. She appears to be having one of her attacks."

"Where are you speaking from?"

"Thirty-nine Stonehurst Gardens."

"I'm terribly sorry," I said. "I can't possibly come all that way. You'll have to get somebody else."

"But I don't know anybody else. You always attend her."

"Well, I really am frightfully sorry, Mr Butterworth, but I'm afraid you'll have to find somebody locally."

"There's no chance of you coming? She does seem awfully queer."

"Don't be unreasonable," I said. "It would take me all night to get there."

"Well… If you won't, you won't."

"Terribly sorry and all that. I'm sure you'll get hold of somebody."

"Just as you say…"

"Bye," I said cheerily and promptly fell once more into a deep sleep.

In the morning Sylvia said: "Why on earth did you refuse to go and see Mrs Butterworth?" And realisation suddenly and horribly dawned.

"My God!" I said. "I thought we were still in Limmering. What did I say?"

"You said he'd have to get somebody locally. You couldn't possibly go all that way."

Stonehurst Gardens was the next road to my own.

"What a damned silly thing to do," I said. "Old Butterworth must have thought I was mad. I must pop round this morning and apologise."

But Mr Butterworth was my first patient in the surgery. He looked at me oddly and shuffled about on the chair.

"Are you feeling all right, Doctor?" he said by way of greeting. I got the impression that he wasn't too happy to be alone in the room with me.

I explained what had happened.

"What must you have thought?" I said when I'd finished.

"Well, to tell you the truth," Mr Butterworth said, "I thought for a moment that I'd gone potty. When you said you couldn't possibly come all that way. I mean it's not more than three minutes on foot. Anyway it was all right. Mrs Butterworth pulled out of it after about five minutes, so I gave her one of the tablets and she went to sleep."

"All's well that ends well, then," I said brightly. "I do hope you understand."

"Oh I understand," Mr Butterworth said, making for the door. But judging by the pitying glance he shot at me as he left I wasn't too sure that he did.

During the rest of a busy week which I felt well able to cope with after the resuscitating sea breezes of Limmering, I found time to draft what I hoped was a comprehensive and appealing advertisement for the services of an assistant. When I had got the phrasing to my satisfaction, and I'm sure Lord Tennyson had not such trouble with composition, I forwarded it to the *Medical Journal* for insertion the following week.

In the small hours of the morning on the day before it was due to appear in print, the Reverend Barker had another heart attack. I was out for three hours and had just got back to bed with the prayer that he would last until the morning, with the drugs I had given him when the phone rang again.

Sylvia said: "Oh, you poor darling," from the snugness of her blankets, and I lifted the receiver.

A voice said "Hallo" in tones more of excitement than of panic.

"Hallo," I said.

"I've got it!"

"You've got what?"

"Old Meakins' job. I'm a Consultant."

"Faraday!"

"You said I could ring you."

"Do you know what time it is?"

"You said 'any time'. I remember distinctly. And I'm off to Switzerland in the morning. I can't believe it. Can I come round?"

"No you can't. Go to bed."

"I wouldn't be able to sleep."

"Well, knock up some poor old GP for a sleeping-pill."

"You bad-tempered old sod."

"So would you be. Cheerio."

"Where are you going?"

"To sleep. Where did you think? And Faraday?"

"Yes?"

"Congratulations. I really am pleased."

"You can show your appreciation in the approved manner."

"What's that?"

"Send me some patients."

"Harley Street?"

"Where else? I'll let you know the number. Go back to bye-byes. Sorry if I disturbed you, Sylvia too."

"Any time," I said. "Good night."

Four

Even to my bleary eyes it looked good. 'Assistant required, attractive London suburb, live-out, obstetrics, possible view, salary according to experience.'

It hardly seemed possible. No time at all seemed to have passed since I was running a nicotine-stained finger down the columns of the same *Medical Journal* for hospital jobs in places ranging from Scunthorpe to West Fife, whose meagre salary barely kept one in cigarettes. Was it possible that in so few years I had graduated from an under-nourished, underpaid, overworked House Physician to an amply-fed, thinning-haired GP, sufficiently prosperous to be contemplating paying away a large portion of his income to an assistant?

Caroline, reading the advertisement over my shoulder and breathing down my neck, said: "I can't see where the 'view' comes into it."

"View to Partnership. If the practice increases sufficiently in size to warrant it. Sit down and eat your yoghurt, there's a good girl."

She removed her bosom from my ear and sat down to the yoghurt and orange juice that was her favourite breakfast.

"I hope you get a cute-looking one," she said. "It would be nice to have somebody cute around the place."

"I'm really more interested in his medical qualifications," I said. "I'm afraid cuteness comes at the bottom of the list of requirements."

"Well, if you need any assistance with character assessment remember I'm a Sociology student and I've had a great deal of experience."

"I'm sure you have," Sylvia said, cutting Peter's toast for him.

"I can sum people up in a moment," Caroline leaned across the table and looked at me over the tops of her glasses. "Have you ever studied the relationship between Physique and Character?" She wagged a finger at me. "By character, of course, I mean the totality of all possibilities of affective and voluntary reaction of any given individual, as they come out in the course of his development, that is to say, what he inherits plus the following exogenous factors: bodily influences, psychic education, milieu…"

Penny said: "Thank-God-for-my-nice-breakfast-please-may-I-get-down?"

"Yes, run and do your teeth; you too Peter." Sylvia smiled at Caroline. "So sorry for the interruption."

"Not at all." Caroline rounded on Sylvia. "As an illustration of this relationship you have only to look at yourself. Now at a glance I would classify you as an Asthenico-Athletic type."

"Hey, wait a minute," I said. I wasn't going to have her getting at Sylvia; "I can't see any plank-like flat chest, outstanding shoulder bones, enteroptotic pendulant stomach…"

"I was referring to the healthy Schizothyme whilst you are talking about the diseased or schizoid personality." Caroline said, undaunted. "You must learn to escape from the narrowness of the psychiatric outlook. You are looking at the world through asylum spectacles."

"Indeed I am not," I said. "Not yet at any rate."

"To get back to Sylvia here. By examining the external architecture you will discover the psychic impulses."

"Like a church?" Sylvia said.

Caroline ignored her. "Typical szhizophrene contours: egg-shaped face with angular profile and slender body. We know that her whole nervous system is tender, she is subject to subtle changes of mood, and depressions, retains an atmosphere of distance, is a slave to aesthetic detail…"

I could see the glint of battle in Sylvia's eyes. She said: "That's terribly interesting, Caroline. Why don't you tell us something about yourself?"

"Oh me and the Doc here have quite a different type of architecture," Caroline said. "We're what you'd call pyknics or cyclothymes, not to be confused with the over-fed asthene. Although we happen to belong to the same morphological group, however, our characteristics are not entirely similar. Take me for instance: good-hearted, sunny-friendliness, knack of getting on easily with people, sociability with a tendency to love of comfort, a lack of tension, of pathos and idealism; in short an average cyclothyme of moderate emotionality. Now Doc here…"

"If you don't mind," I said, "I have to start the surgery. Tell Sylvia. I'm sure she'll be fascinated to learn what lies beneath my architecture."

"Unfortunately I've already discovered," Sylvia said, standing up. "If you'll excuse me I have to take the children to school."

"Sure," Caroline said, not in the least put out. She smiled at Sylvia. "One thing I missed out in my assessment of you, dear. The polite, sensitive schizothyme usually has one fault in an otherwise pure and lofty character; that is a violent antipathy towards individual objects."

Sylvia looked her in the eye. "And how does the individual object react to the antipathy?"

"It has no effect whatever," Caroline said sweetly, "on a cyclothyme."

It was quite a relief to get into the surgery. As I walked through the packed waiting-room into my consulting room I thought how pleasant it would be when I had my assistant and would be able both to get through the work in half the time and to give better attention to each patient.

After a disturbed night a session such as I now faced seemed a Herculean task. You could not compare the tired business man with the weary doctor. Whilst the former, after a night out, might bark at his secretary, offend his customers or make a hash of a deal, the latter could, if he were not on his guard, fail to make a diagnosis which could result in the loss of life. At the best of times a morning surgery in which one had often to see some forty patients was an ordeal.

The first few were usually not too much of an effort. One could even manage a bright smile.

"Good morning, Mrs Smith."

"Mornin'."

"Nice and early this morning."

"I bin 'ere since ar-past. I wanted to be the first. Gotta go down the shop."

"Good. What's the trouble?"

"It's me stomick."

"What's the matter with your stomick...er stomach?"

"I can't keep nuthink down."

"You mean you vomit after food?"

"It's not me food. I never eat nuthink. I can't."

"I see. What about your weight?"

"I dunno."

"Have you noticed that your skirt is tight or loose?"

"Loose."

I wrote down 'Loss of weight.'

"It's me sister's," Mrs Smith said.

I scratched it out.

"Sleeping well?"

"When 'e lets me."

"What did you have for breakfast?"

"Sossidges."

"I thought you said you never eat anything?"

"I never said of a mornin' I didn't."

"All right, Mrs Smith. Get undressed and let me examine you."

"I only wanted a stomick bottle."

"I can't give you any treatment without examining you."

"I can't. Not today."

"Why not?"

She simpered. "It's not convenient."

I stood up. "Well, come back next week, and we'll find out what the trouble is."

Mrs Smith remained seated. "Well, can I 'ave me bottle?"

"What for?"

"Me stomick. Can't keep nuthink down."

I sighed and wrote out a prescription.

The edge had worn off my smile by the time the next patient came in. Oddly enough her name was also Smith. It was a coincidence I frequently noticed. If one Smith came she was often followed by one, two or even three more in the same surgery. If a Mrs Brown attended, she would be followed by a Mrs Green, Mrs Black and Mrs White. It was the same with visits. On the day that 24, The Close rang for a call, it was not uncommon for numbers 22 and 26, unknown to each other, to do so too.

The second Mrs Smith considered herself as intelligent as the first Mrs Smith was uninformed. She dragged in with her a small child who instantly had my sympathy.

"Hilary has earache, Doctor, for the second time this week and it's not good enough. I'm afraid it's going to develop into an otitis media and I'm extremely worried. I'd like a letter to the hospital."

I preferred to deal with a dozen of the first Mrs Smith's than one of the second who before she stepped into the surgery had made the diagnosis and prescribed treatment.

"Come here, Hilary," I said to the child, "and let me have a look in your ear."

"Now mind you don't cry, Hilary," Mrs Smith said to the child who had had no intention of crying; "be a brave girl for the doctor. It won't hurt very much."

Aloud I said: "It won't hurt at all." Beneath my breath I muttered rude things at Mrs Smith for upsetting the child who had now started to scream with terror.

Above the din Mrs Smith said: "I know you can't be too careful with ears. My niece in Birmingham was in hospital for six months with an unresolved middle ear infection and the surgeon said 'Mrs Stockbridge', that's my sister, 'if this had only been diagnosed earlier...' "

I handed her the orange bead I had extracted from Hilary's ear.

"Good morning, Mr Roach," I said.

"Eh?" He cupped his ear.

"Nothing," I yelled. "Sit down!"

After the third patient the morning ebullience began to show some signs of wear. After the thirtieth it was almost impossible to bring the same freshness to the consultation, to give the impression that the patient occupying the chair was the one and only with whom one had to deal. Yet it was what was expected.

The difference between the business man and the doctor was this. With business one could delegate, prevaricate, no one would be any the worse. In General Practice, with each consultation one gave a little of oneself; in order to help the patients one had to. Thirty little pieces of oneself amounted to quite a lot of wear and tear; add to this anything between five and twenty-five visits, when one had in addition the physical exertion of driving, getting in and out of the car, and running up and down stairs, then another twenty or thirty consultations in the evening surgery, followed possibly by one or two evening and night calls. It was not surprising I had come to the conclusion I could not continue at this pace. I looked forward to the coming of my assistant.

On the way to Essex to see the Reverend Barker I considered the good news with which my friend Faraday had seen fit to disturb us in the middle of the night. At last he had reached Consultant status. Realising, now I had time to think about it, its implications, I understood his excitement and forgave him for rushing to the telephone the very minute he knew. It was something to shout about. Faraday, with whom I had been a student, was the same age as I and about ten times as brainy, yet for years he had been hanging round on the penultimate step of the medical ladder, not because he had not the ability to reach the top, but because there were simply not enough Consultant posts to go round to the eagerly outstretched hands of the hard-working, poorly remunerated Senior Registrars. Faraday had waited for years but he was one of the more fortunate ones and still young to have achieved Consultant status. He had reached the top and no one deserved it more. I smiled to myself as I tried to imagine Faraday behind a desk in Harley Street. The imagination balked. Faraday was a skinny, lanky chap who looked ten years younger than he was and as though he were going to fall to pieces at any moment. He was handsome in a loose-limbed, amiable way and had a boyish grin that brought girls flocking. Anybody looking less like a Consultant Neuro-logist was difficult to imagine; the impression he gave was more one of an irresponsible young man selling pop-records. In addition to finding him some patients for private consultations I could see that I would also have to give him some friendly advice.

Whilst thinking of Faraday I considered my own career. I had originally chosen General Practice in order to earn enough money to marry Sylvia but I had realised years ago that this was my proper niche. I would never have had the singleness of purpose to stick it out, apparently getting nowhere as Faraday had, in one hospital after another. I was too conscious of the years slipping by and wanted too much too soon. And it wasn't only the material side; I was aware, and it had nothing to do with conceit, that the broad field of General Practice suited the way my mind worked. It was easy for me to see things as on a wide screen, to take into account all possibilities, side issues and family histories, to apply any native wit and modicum of intelligence I might have, in addition to the knowledge of medicine I had learned and acquired over the years, and to come up with a diagnosis. It helped too that I was interested in people. After eight years, during the course of which I had dealt with many hundreds of patients, I knew in a second who was telling the truth and who was not, who was sick and who imagined he was, whom I could help and whom I could not. The study was a fascinating one and one of which I knew I could never tire. I suppose that this was the answer to the question I had put to myself 'what did I want?' I wanted more time to practise better medicine. The mass-production stuff I was forced to now was no good for me and certainly anything but in the best interests of the patients. I imagined scores of assistants all over the country penning letters in answer to my advertisement and I could hardly wait for the morning's post.

The condition of the Reverend Barker seemed slightly improved. He lay propped up in bed and smiled as I came in.

"I can't tell you how sorry I am for bringing you out last night," he said quietly. "It's such a long way for you to come."

"All part of the service," I said cheerily as I took his blood-pressure. "One gets used to it." I hoped I sounded convincing. Of course it wasn't true. Getting out of bed in the middle of the night was something I could never get used to no matter how many times I did it, and that was pretty often. On each occasion it was just as much an effort and a penance as it had been the very first time.

When I had finished my examination the Reverend Barker raised one eyebrow and looked at me.

"Another day of grace?"

I turned away to put my things back into my case. "I hope there will be many, many more."

"Everything that was precious before becomes doubly so." He looked out of the window. "The trees with their bare branches, waiting for the spring, the sun, the birds, the rain. The sound of children getting up in the morning, your wife's familiar footstep on the stairs, the way she smiles at you...the bounty of the Lord is endless."

I thought of the entirely different things the majority of my patients regarded as the bounty of the Lord. Number one on the list came the Telly, without which life became unbearable; this was followed closely by the washing-machine, the car and the spin-dryer.

"The wonder to me," the Reverend said, "is not that we die so young but that we live so long. When you think of the delicate mechanism of the body, into which the Almighty breathes life, functioning so faultlessly day after day until He recalls it. But of course it must seem even more of a marvel to you – you understand the working of the thing."

I smiled. "Sufficient at any rate to attend to the plumbing."

"You underestimate yourself."

I shook my head. "That's all it amounts to when you consider it."

The Reverend said: "The analogy was yours but I wonder if the day will come when backing the doctor, as the hardware shops back the plumber, there will be wholesale fittings depots supplying new parts and replacements. Hearts, lungs, livers, kidneys – all on the Health Service of course."

I laughed. The Reverend had always had a keen sense of humour.

"It's not outside the realms of possibility," I said, and turned to get my overcoat from the chair. "I mean when you consider the rate of scientific progress…"

With one arm in my coat I faced the bed again. My back had been turned only for a moment but in that time something had happened to the Reverend Barker. Just now he had been smiling happily, now his head was lolling unnaturally on his chest and his hands were still on the blankets. I ran to him, calling his name and leaving my coat in a heap on the floor. There was no response, no pulse, no breath that I could detect. Alone in the room with the sudden horrid silence of death, I injected a stimulant as quickly as I could into the heart muscle. It was a token only. It rarely worked and this time was no exception.

I could hardly believe that in mid-conversation, in the space of a few seconds, less than the flap of a bird's wings, the miracle, for the Reverend Barker, had ended. His heart had ceased to function and despite our facile talk there were no replacements available.

I put my things into my case slowly, trying to compose in my head a few sentences which would break the news with the least degree of shock to Mrs Barker. I heard someone coming up. "The wonder of…your wife's footsteps on the stairs." Her tread was light but he could no longer hear it.

I met her outside the door. She was holding a basket of fruit and smiling.

"People are so kind," she said. "You can't imagine. This is the second today and old Mrs Bentley made some beef-tea and brought it round herself when she can hardly walk, poor dear…" She looked at my face. "There's something wrong!"

"I'm afraid…there is."

She said nothing for a moment and I sensed the agony of the future, the loneliness and the struggle passing through her head. Then she remembered the God whose Will she firmly believed it was.

"The children will enjoy the fruit," she said very slowly. "I'll take it downstairs then come up to my husband."

"Would you like me to call a neighbour?" I said.

Two single tears were on her cheeks. "I am not afraid."

I had long ago grown used to death but I still hated to lose patients, in particular those I had grown fond of and friendly with, like the Reverend Barker. I was familiar with death but had, of course, not solved its mystery. I could not help wondering, as I drove towards home, whether it was indeed as simple as the Reverend Barker had with his faith, believed. Was he now resting in the arms of his Maker? Would I ever know?

Five

Caroline, dressed in trousers so tight they looked like purple skin, picked up the morning post and brought it into the morning-room where Sylvia and I were finishing our coffee.

"Quick," I said, anxious to see how many replies I had had to my advertisement, "give them to me."

I skimmed through the envelopes examining the postmarks: Blackpool, Glasgow, Huddersfield, County Tyrone, West Hartlepool, Broadstairs, several from London...

With the paper-knife, supplied with their compliments and advice on the newest treatment of scabies, by Credo-Medicals, I eagerly slit open the envelope of the first of my replies.

DEAR MADAM,
Further to your enquiry for a Sylph-Form strapless bra, we are pleased to inform you that we have just had a delivery...

I looked again at the envelope, then handed it to Sylvia. "Sorry, Sweetie," I said. "It's such shocking writing, the Mrs looks just like Dr."

The next letter was not from a prospective assistant either. It was from a House Agent and stated that in answer to our recent enquiry he was in a position to offer us a number of desirable properties, details of which he had much pleasure in enclosing.

47

"Sylvia," I said.

"Mm?"

"Aren't you rather putting the cart before the horse?"

"How do you mean?"

I waved the letter at her. "Badgering House Agents before we've even a sniff of an assistant."

"Is that from Jessup's? Let me see."

I had another look at the letter. "I suppose you told Mr Jessup that money was no object? There's nothing here under three times as much as we could possibly afford to pay."

"Well, I did mention that we wanted something really nice. We do, don't we?"

"Indeed we do."

"Well, there we are then," Sylvia said brightly and I handed her the list of houses Mr Jessup was under the mistaken impression we were in a financial position to consider.

"Exciting," Sylvia said. "I adore looking at houses." She held out her hand. "You'd better give me some of those replies to read or you'll never get into the surgery."

"Nosey," I said, giving her a few of the envelopes.

"Nobody ever writes to me."

We each opened a letter simultaneously.

"A female," I said, reading mine. "Useless. What's yours?"

"Male from Middlesbrough with four children."

"He'd never feed them on the salary."

My next was a newly qualified youth who said he would like to 'try' General Practice. I didn't think my patients would stand for an assistant still wet behind the ears. The next was a man of fifty. I wondered what he was doing still applying for not very well-paid assistantship jobs and, feeling sorry for him, put him on the pile of rejects.

"Here's one that speaks Urdu," Sylvia said.

"That would be useful."

There was a German who sent twelve pages of neatly typed information about himself under relevant headings and seemed only to have omitted details of when his mother began mixed-feeding; a hastily scrawled note from a chap who said nothing at all about himself but that he'd like to live in the district because he had a girl friend near by; one who felt sure he could give every satisfaction but whose qualifications were from some University I had never heard of and another whose signature I was quite unable to read.

In this batch at any rate the quantity by far outweighed the quality.

I picked out the two or three possibles and leaving Sylvia and Caroline to read them over again, started work.

During the morning I tested out some of the patients.

"I'm getting an assistant shortly, Mrs Brown, to help me with the work," I said.

"Quite right, Doctor, so you should," Mrs Brown said sympathetically. "Of course we'll come to you though."

"Of course," I said.

"I shall have an assistant soon," I said to Mr Walsh, "to make the practice more efficient."

"A very sensible decision, Doctor, if I may say so," said Mr Walsh. "It's quite obviously too much for you on your own. I shall continue to consult you though. So will the wife and kids. We've got used to you after all this time."

Mr Dodge, the postman, said: "You know my case, Doc; wouldn't be the same with someone else. Good idea though for them as aren't particular."

In the course of the whole morning I was unable to find anyone who wasn't 'particler'. Perhaps the idea of an assistant was not such a brilliant one as I had thought.

Sylvia, as usual, brought me to my senses.

"You know quite well you can't carry on like this," she said. "It will take time but if you find somebody nice the patients will eventually get used to it. They'll have to."

"Or change to somebody else," I said, visions of my practice, built up patient by patient with the sweat of my brow, gradually disintegrating.

"They won't change," Sylvia said. "At least, even with an assistant, they'll have half a chance of seeing you. If they change to someone else they won't be able to see you at all!"

There was, I supposed, something in what Sylvia said although I had the uncomfortable feeling that somewhere in her argument there was the twisted application of feminine logic.

I did my visits in high spirits, all the time looking forward to going home to see what the second post would bring in the way of replies. Now that I had made up my mind about this thing I wanted to lose no time in putting it into practice.

At twelve-thirty I opened the front door. As well as some dozen letters on the floor, there was stacked up in the hall a mountain of luggage. I counted three trunks, two suitcases, four packing cases, one of which was opened, a record-player, fishing-rod, two tennis rackets, bag of golf-clubs and a set of dumb-bells.

Sylvia came out of the kitchen.

"What's going on?" I said. "Are we moving out already?"

"No," Sylvia smiled sweetly, "your Cousin Caroline is moving in. She'll give you lunch too, Sweetie. I have to go up to town and I'm late!"

She gave me a kiss on my forehead and was out of the door before I could collect my wits or ask what time she would be back.

"Hy, Doc," Caroline said, coming down the stairs. "My baggage has arrived."

"So I see."

She kneeled by the opened packing case and took out an armful of magazines called *Glamour*.

"There's no cause for alarm," she said, noticing my expression. "I'll soon get this little lot shifted."

"Little lot?"

"Sure. I didn't have too much sent on. I left the rest with Anty in Frinton."

"How long did you say you were in England for?"

"Few months." She was piling more *Glamour* magazines into her arms.

"What are those for?"

She looked surprised.

"Back numbers!"

"I see." I looked around. "You fish?"

"Uh-huh."

"Play golf?"

"Sure."

"What's your handicap?"

"Eight," she said modestly.

I swallowed. "We must have a game some time."

"Thursday?" she said. Thursday was my half-day.

"Well...possibly. What are these for?" I kicked the Indian clubs.

"Bust," Caroline said.

I nodded. It seemed to me that she had more than enough of that commodity already.

"Tones 'em up, stops them from flopping. All-round muscular improvement."

"Good idea," I said. "Look, Caroline, just let me read these letters, then I'll help you get this lot upstairs."

"Upstairs?"

"To your room."

"I was wondering," Caroline said. "I didn't get a chance to ask Sylvia, but I thought the *Glamours* and the record-player in the morning-room, the clubs and the rod in the hall closet; I wasn't sure about the trunks..."

I wasn't sure either but I had a pretty shrewd idea of what Sylvia was going to say to all this.

"...I don't believe in cluttering the sleeping quarters," Caroline was saying. "It's unhealthy."

51

If there was one thing which occupied Caroline's thoughts more than Sex it was 'Health'.

She had started on the first day of what looked as if it was to be a prolonged visit by removing the pillows, eiderdown, rug, chair and curtains in her bedroom. We had found them in a heap in the corridor.

"Allergy," Caroline explained. "Allergic to feathers, household dust and disintegrating materials", she kicked the curtains.

"Just a minute," Sylvia said. "Those curtains for the spare bedroom were new last year. They can't possibly be disintegrating."

"Macroscopically no," Caroline said. "However, minute particles, invisible to the naked eye, are continually sloughing off and irritating the nasal mucosa. If it's all the same to you I prefer bare boards and the minimum of furniture."

"There's always the garage," Sylvia said. But fortunately I don't think Caroline heard her.

Then there were her pills. She must have swallowed some twenty or more during the course of any one day. Their functions, or supposed functions, varied. Apart from the vitamin pills without which she was unable to sleep at night, pills without which she was unable to rouse herself from her morning torpor; pills to calm her nerves, pills to alert them; pills to assist her bowels to function, pills to prevent them from doing so too frequently; pills to make her eat, pills to take away her appetite; slimming pills and body-building pills, pills to give her confidence in herself, and pills to make her pleasant to be 'near to'. She had a pill for everything and for everything there was a pill. I don't know how she remembered which were for what, she had so many of them.

"What do you think would happen to you if you threw the whole lot away?" I said to her one day.

"Oh I couldn't," she said. "Back home we all take pills."

And I believed there was something in what she said. She didn't go round sniffing 'snow' or taking the odd draw at a 'reefer' but she was almost as much of a drug addict as those who did. She had been conditioned into her pills and could not visualise life without them. She was only eighteen and it seemed to me a sad state of affairs. I dreaded to think what she would be like by the time she was forty.

And the pills were not all. Her food fads drove Sylvia nearly mad. In addition to her 'laxative' cereals, wholewheat bread and yoghurt which she swallowed by the pint, she counted her calory intake with a sort of ready-reckoner she carried around with her and if her calculations told her she had reached her limits for the day, that was that. Nothing would induce her to eat the steak and chips or fruit flan Sylvia had prepared for dinner and she would sit at the table nibbling a lettuce leaf completely impervious to Sylvia's glares.

Neither did it end there. Not satisfied with her interest in the workings of her own body, with special reference to its refuelling, she turned her attention to the children and myself.

Sylvia, Caroline had announced one day at dinner, was slowly killing me. The murderess bridled. The only absolving factor, Caroline went on to say, was that the crime was being committed in ignorance. There was no malice aforethought.

Sylvia had looked at me across the table.

"He looks fit enough to me," she said to Caroline. "Eats like a horse, sleeps like a log…"

"Ah!" Caroline said, "that's just the point. He's neither a horse nor a log but a middle-aged male…"

"Hey, wait a minute," I said; "since when has thirty-seven been middle-aged?"

But Caroline went on: "…you have to watch his blood cholesterol."

She thrust a finger in the air at Sylvia.

"Do you cook his food in corn oil instead of animal or vegetable derivatives? No!" She answered her own question and two fingers went up.

"Do you watch his cholesterol intake, eggs, chocolate, butter, cheese? No!"

A third finger went up but Sylvia had had enough of the indictment.

"Caroline," she said, and I had rarely seen her so angry. "He happens to be *my* husband and *my* responsibility and I'd be happy if you'd mind your own business and get on with your 'dinner'."

Caroline was tucking in to a plate of raw carrots at the time. She was not in the least put out.

"Medical evidence has proved conclusively," she said equably, but since the telephone rang at that moment with the news that Mrs Barnes had dropped her baby on the kitchen floor I never heard what it was that medical evidence had proved so conclusively that ignorance of it might affect my entire future.

As far as the children were concerned Caroline maintained that on the diet on which we kept them they would be toothless, listless, malformed dullards by the time they were eighteen. Having heard what she had to say on the subject of what they ate, when they ate it, how, when, on what, and where they slept, the frequency, and with what they brushed their teeth, we decided to take a chance.

Had she known about the NSPCC, I have no doubt that Caroline would have had no hesitation in putting our names in front of them. We didn't enlighten her.

At five-thirty I came out of the surgery for a moment while Mrs Passmore was struggling with her corset to see if Sylvia had returned. I found her in the bathroom, kneeling before the bath in which there was a twin at either end, and stood in the doorway for a moment, watching them, consumed with love.

Sylvia, still in her town clothes over which she had tied a white apron, and unaware of my presence, looked like the model she had been when I married her, but a model brought to life by happiness and domesticity. By *haute couture* standards she would never have made the grade; a few strands of hair had straggled down from her elegant hairstyle, she had rolled up the sleeves of her silk shirt and there was soap on her face; also, unforgivable sin, she was smiling.

I stood watching them, my blessings, well aware that this was the other side of the coin, one of the compensations of General Practice. I did not have to leave the house in the mornings before my children were up and arrive home only in time to kiss their sleeping faces. I could communicate with or embrace my wife at frequent intervals during the day as we did not have, as most couples did, to renew our acquaintanceship each evening after dinner. We were dependent upon each other in a way that sometimes made me a little afraid but it was a sweet relationship I would not have changed for all the golden carrots the world could dangle before me. We were so used to being together that if Sylvia went out for the day I missed her horribly and envisaged her the victim of countless horrid street accidents, and if I was too long on a call I would arrive home to find Sylvia gazing anxiously out of the window. We were so used to talking to each other it made us lazy in talking to other people who did not understand us half so well, and it no longer surprised us when one of us voiced thoughts that at just that moment the other had been thinking. We knew each other better than many other husbands and wives dared to or cared to but discovered that the more we plumbed the greater and more satisfying were the depths.

It was Peter who saw me first.

"Thith ith a thubmarine," he said, referring to the soap. "Penny ith a battleship."

"No surgery?" Sylvia said.

"I just wanted to make sure you were back."

"You'll never guess who I met in Pont Street…"

"I'll pop out again in a minute," I said, "and you can tell me. I left Mrs Passmore doing battle with her corset."

Six

"Doctor, you're a saint!" Miss Chudley, sitting up in bed in mob cap and pink woolly bed-jacket, said it as though she meant it and I believed she did.

Miss Chudley was an inheritance.

I had often looked with envy at those large, old fashioned, chauffeur-driven Rolls-Royces one saw sailing along from time to time, in which, sitting up in a sort of bed arrangement at the back were a variety of old ladies, shouting imperious instructions down speaking-tubes.

Whenever I came across such an equipage I wondered how one obtained such an obviously wealthy, obviously private, obviously in-need-of-constant-attention patient. I never thought the day would come when I, humble suburban practitioner, would have one of my very own.

Miss Chudley was bequeathed to me by my friend Doctor Archibald Compton when he emigrated to Canada a year earlier. She was handed over, together with several hundred less extraordinary patients, a few rusty syringes and a pair of scales Archie no longer had any use for. How Archie wormed his way into the Chudley *ménage* in the first place I had never found out. That he would find no similar charge in Canada I was convinced. The Chudley set-up was as English as round, red pillar boxes, kidneys for breakfast and early morning tea.

Miss Chudley was a law unto herself. She favoured the almost extinct role of 'grand old eccentric' and she played it to perfection.

Apart from the hearse-like car into which she was helped each day for her stately outing by Withers the chauffeur and Gregg who had been her personal maid since the year dot and was now her companion, she took pride in the fact that in her ninety-odd years upon this earth she had never blasphemed, taken the name of the Lord her God in vain, spoken on the telephone or touched money; she had a very poor opinion of those who did. Finding herself in what she considered the ill-bred world which had emerged from the holocaust of two major wars, Miss Chudley clung, as far as she was able, to the old order. She refused to acknowledge a state of affairs in which the emphasis was on 'Instant this', 'Instant that', and 'Do-it-yourself' and created her own empire in which such oddities as button-hooks, goffering irons and the black-leading of grates still persisted.

In a way I admired her for not succumbing, as had most of the Grandmas I knew, to the indignity of the Cha-Cha, the soullessness of the push button, and the sloth of the drip-dry. Not that Miss Chudley, of course, was a Grandma. She had never married, she told me, not for want of opportunity but because she considered such a state to be vulgar, and had now outlived an entire battery of relations who had passed on, both through the exigencies of war and the inexorable processes of natural selection.

Miss Chudley had the constitution of an ox. Apart from the strain imposed upon her various organs by the years, there was nothing the matter with her and my regular visits to her were purely of a routine nature. Had I saved her from a nasty death or relieved her from a lifetime of suffering she could not however have been more grateful.

For my slight attentions, my few words of encouragement, she sanctified me. But that was not all. Each time I visited her,

Miss Chudley indicated, in no uncertain terms, that when she died I was to benefit from her will. She owned, she said, a castle in Scotland, a Cornish village and countless properties in London, the income from which was steadily swelling various scarcely-touched accounts. She had no friends, having outlived them all, did not care for dogs or cats, and loved, she said, only Withers, Gregg and myself. She reiterated constantly that when she passed on the three of us would have no cause for complaint.

It was the kind of thing that was constantly happening to doctors who were responsible for the care of elderly patients. In my brief career I had already collected, as bequests, a hideous carved mirror I had been foolish enough to admire in an unthinking moment, a painting of a shiny, ill-proportioned Madonna clutching a child no larger than a tadpole (Mr Baker knew how interested I was in Art, Mrs Baker said), and a silver sugar-bowl now in regular use and which we irreverently referred to by the name of its donor, one Emily Wilks (carcinoma of the colon).

I paid little attention to Miss Chudley's assurances of my future expectations, regarding them as no more than the idle chit-chat to which as a family doctor I had frequently to listen. I had not even mentioned them to Sylvia.

To Miss Chudley I was a saint. To Mrs MacConnal I was an ill-mannered, heartless, inconsiderate, steel-fingered, slovenly, lazy, ignorant wretch who had, however, been sufficiently quick-witted to pull the wool over the examiners' eyes for long enough to become qualified as a medical practitioner.

The odd part about this was that for Miss Chudley I did nothing at all; my visits to her could be more accurately described as social rather than medical; while to Mrs MacConnal I gave more time, energy, patience and medical skill than to any other single one of my patients. It was no exaggeration of the facts that it was only through my efforts over a period of the last three or four years, that she was still alive. I had been in practice too long to expect anyone to be grateful for what was done for them (we're payin', aren't we?) but the abuse I received from the anything but ladylike lips of Mrs MacConnal was going a bit far in the opposite direction.

She lived in what had once been a beautifully fresh, clean Council flat at the top of a six-storied block with no lift and which she had, with the aid of her soak of a husband and three children, lost no time in converting into a reasonable facsimile of a pigsty. The MacConnals lived by a simple, tripartite, negative creed. No work, no cooking, no washing. They lived on National Assistance and chips, and wallowed in their own filth.

Mrs MacConnal suffered from a form of cardiac asthma, attacks of which came on, as was typical in the condition, in the early hours of the morning. I was usually summoned by a neighbour, who only in extreme emergency could be prevailed upon to have anything to do with the filthy family – MacConnal in his 'small hour' stupor being generally unrousable.

I would find Mrs MacConnal desperately ill, literally fighting for breath, lying in her underwear among stinking bedclothes. The treatment was the immediate administration of morphia and possibly oxygen and sometimes venesection was necessary.

The name 'MacConnal' ejected urgently into the darkness, after the drop of the pennies at the pressing of button 'A', always caused my heart to sink, and I knew there would be little more sleep that night.

During the course of my nocturnal visits to the MacConnal flat I said nothing, unless it was to one of the grimy children. Mrs MacConnal was usually in no state for light conversation and her husband in no state for anything at all.

In the morning call that followed these nightly high-jinks I had plenty to say to all. Before I uttered a word, however, I would throw open all the windows, which was not as easy as it sounds, in an attempt to replace with a little sweet air the indescribable smell of mingled chips, beer, stale urine and the general odour of unwashed bodies.

Mrs MacConnal would shiver and cower under the bedclothes.

"I'll catch me death," she'd whine.

"You're far more likely to die from the smell in this place than from a little fresh air," I'd say. "I can't breathe if you can. You should be thoroughly ashamed of yourself."

On the morning after one of my night visits to Mrs MacConnal I could count on being confronted with at least three patients demanding attention.

On one occasion I had just finished examining Mrs MacConnal, who was now completely recovered from her attack of the previous night, when she delved under the grey sheets and came up with a small baby.

"What's he doing down there?" I said, surprised.

" 'Is eyes is sticky," Mrs MacConnal said, "so I kep' 'im in the dark. I didn't want 'im to be struck blind."

"How long have his eyes been sticky?"

"Fortnight or three weeks."

"You haven't had him down there all the time?"

"Oh no. Only this morning. They was more stickier this morning."

"Why haven't I see him before?" I demanded, "if he's had sore eyes for three weeks?"

"Yer not so keen on comin'. Yer never come when Mrs Wallace's Charlie got a 'ook in 'is 'and."

"Coming?" I said. "For sticky eyes? You know perfectly well what the surgery hours are."

"Ooh, I couldn't fetch 'im down."

"Why not?"

"Me feet."

"What's the matter with your feet?"

"They're ill."

"You'd better let me have a look at them then."

She thrust a pair of sickeningly dirty feet out from the bedclothes. I didn't touch them.

"They look all right to me."

"I need some ligament."

"Who said so?"

"Mrs Jones. The lady give 'er some for the harthritis."

"You haven't got arthritis. I can't see anything the matter with your feet."

"I never *arst* you to look at me feet."

"You did."

"I never. You arst me why I never fetched the baby down and I said…"

"All right, all right." I took out my prescription pad and wrote up something for the baby's eyes, knowing that if I waited for Mrs MacConnal to bring it to the surgery the poor child would be very much worse than it was now.

"These are drops," I said. "Put one drop in each eye four times a day. And," I said, aware that I was wasting my breath, "you have to be careful. This condition is most infectious."

"I know," Mrs MacConnal said with a superior air.

"How?"

"Brenda!" Mrs MacConnal screeched, and in answer to the summons a five-year-old came in wearing only a vest which barely covered her umbilicus. There was chocolate on her face.

"Show the doctor yer eyes!" Mrs MacConnal said triumphantly.

I wrote another prescription. "And keep their bottles separately," I said with no enthusiasm. Before I signed my name I said:

"What about the other child?"

"Alfie? 'E's inside."

"Why isn't he at school?"

Mrs MacConnal looked hurt. "On account of 'is eyes!"

It was time I went. I had a long list to get through. I was at the door when Mrs MacConnal called me back.

"Oy," she said. "What about me ligament?"

"Come to the surgery," I said, "when you've washed your feet and we'll see about it."

" 'Ow can I when I can't walk?"

"You can walk down to the Three Feathers."

"I'll 'ave the lor on you. I pay me stamp same as Mrs Wallace an yer never come when 'er Charlie got a 'ook in 'is 'and…"

"Mrs MacConnal," I said, "I've been here half the night and I don't intend spending half the morning here as well. If there's anything else you wish to consult me about you can come to the surgery and if you don't try to be a little more co-operative I shall remove the whole lot of you from my list."

I shut the front door and waited for the stream of invective that habitually accompanied me down the stairs. I didn't have long to wait.

"Gettin' too big fer 'is boots 'e is. Never minded comin' when 'e first started. Too 'igh an mighty ter see to anyone's feet. 'Wash yer feet!' 'e says 'an' come an' see me in the surgery…' ooh shut up Alfie or I'll crown yer…where's that bleedin' farther o' yours…?"

Number forty, a quiet, respectable little woman, putting Brasso on her knocker, looked at me sympathetically.

"Gets worse and worse, she does," she said. "A disgrace, that's what she is. 'Er and the kids. A disgrace."

So there I was, saint and sinner and often both in the course of the same day. I was also, according to Sylvia, a chameleon.

Often, while we were having dinner at night, or sitting down afterwards talking, Sylvia would say: "I suppose you've been to the Thorpes today?"

"Yes, I did see the Major," I'd say, surprised. "How do you know?"

"I guessed. You keep saying 'First class! First class!' That can only be Major Thorpe."

It was the same when I'd had a session with Mrs Clatworthy in the surgery. Mrs Clatworthy had something the matter with her larynx which prevented her speaking in anything above a whisper. Whenever I had spent any time with her the next patient invariably had to say:

"I'm terribly sorry, Doctor, I don't know if it's my ears, but I'm afraid I can't hear what you're saying."

After Mr Dawes I laughed like a drain for the rest of the day; and after Basil Partridge from the farm I went round slapping everyone on the back and calling them 'old boy' in a manner completely alien to my customary behaviour.

It was the same with their occupations, and I can only suppose that I must be very susceptible to suggestion.

It was not unusual, during the course of any one evening for me to wonder whether I might not have done better in life had I, instead of taking up medicine, decided to be a greyhound trainer, tin-can manufacturer, or film producer. The choice of careers, of course, varied according to the patients I had seen that day. Twenty-four hours later I would be equally firmly convinced that my vocation lay in travelling in encyclopaedias, breeding bulldogs or growing chrysanthemums.

I suppose it is difficult to walk constantly among the daisies and avoid being dusted by some of the pollen.

Whatever adhered, Sylvia usually managed to brush off.

"You'd be hopeless in business," she'd say. "You can't sit still for five minutes. Can you imagine yourself sitting at a desk all day."

And, of course, neither could I, when I considered it, become really impassioned over bulldogs, or raise any enthusiasm for tin cans.

On Sylvia's insistence we had been looking at houses. That it was still a little premature I knew, but Sylvia had got so carried away by the thought of moving I hadn't the heart to damp her ardour; most of the houses we saw soon did that. If nothing else, our conducted tours round a variety of 'desirable residences' had put us wise both to House Agents and their smudgy eulogies of bargains they had to offer. We were now not only dead cunning but crafty as well, and we had trained ourselves to read between the lines of the roneo'd pages we received with every morning's post.

We now knew that 'conveniently placed for transport' meant that there was a bus-stop right outside the door; and 'secluded spot' that there was none for miles and miles. 'Period house' was a fair indication of ingle-nooks, tiny windows and claustrophobic rooms, while a 'modern residence' was usually one of rows of identical modern residences, distinguishable one from the other only by the hideous variety of the tiled mantelpieces.

We knew that 'part central heating' was one lukewarm radiator in the hall; 'oak-panelled' an entrance so dark that the light was necessary even at mid-day; 'playroom running length of house' (one we had enthusiastically fallen for early on) a small window fitted into one end of the loft, reached by a precarious ladder quite unsuitable for children, and 'well-stocked garden' a couple of overgrown apple trees and some ancient daffodils.

We had now reached the cynical stage and no longer bullied the agent into arranging for our immediate inspection the moment we received particulars of a house.

I was very surprised therefore when I came home on the day before I was to interview my first prospective assistant, to find Sylvia on the doorstep and bubbling with excitement.

"I've seen it," she said, "I've seen it!"

"What?"

"A house. *The* house."

"It can't be any good," I said from the depths of my disillusionment. "And if it is it must be too expensive."

Sylvia's bubble was unburstable. She babbled on about the bathroom, the basins, the cupboards and the kitchen.

"You must come and see it," she said finally, "straight away."

"If it's all the same to you," I said, "I still haven't been to see Mrs Drew's bronchitis or Baby Cuthbert's chicken-pox." I looked at her suspiciously.

"Anyway I haven't heard you mention the price. How much do they want?"

Sylvia's face fell.

"Well, it is rather a lot," she said. "But I expect they'd come down a bit."

"From the look on your face," I said, "we couldn't even manage the bit they'd come down. Out with it. How much?"

Sylvia whispered an astronomic sum.

"You must be crazy," I said.

"It *is* divine!"

"I've no doubt," I said and then, in a weak moment, agreed to go and see it.

Seven

It was two weeks later before I managed to find the time to inspect this gem that Sylvia had discovered. In the first week the people who owned it were away and the house locked up, and in the second week practically every child in the district developed chicken-pox.

Chicken-pox is not a serious complaint. Many mothers were able to cope with it on their own or with the aid of a bottle of calamine lotion. The rest of them kept me on the run. While the first batch of children itched and scratched, anxious parents kept a weather eye on the seconds and thirds. The telephone didn't stop.

"Jennifer has chicken-pox, what about the baby?"

"Susan was going to stay with her Granny and Robert has chicken-pox, is it all right for her to go?"

"How long will it be before we know if Arthur's going to get it?"

"Can Penelope go to school?"

"Jane has chicken-pox, my sister-in-law is pregnant, is it all right if she comes to tea?"

"Richard has one or two blistery spots, Doctor, and today's the day of the House swimming...?"

"Melanie's been awake all night scratching, is there anything I can do?"

"Steven has chicken-pox, Doctor, can my *au pair* go to her classes?"

I had little time to think about houses and even less to consider assistants.

There had been a number of possible replies to my advertisement though, and during the mad rush of the past fortnight I had managed to interview some of the applicants.

Those I saw I didn't take to at all, and one we frightened away before I'd even had a chance to see him.

From the beginning it was a task that I hated. It started with the letters from applicants, all desperately keen. It made me feel sad that men the same age as myself, with similar qualifications and as much, or in many cases more, experience, should still be drifting around, unsettled, receiving ridiculously low salaries and that only here and there.

There were two main reasons for the state in which the authors of the letters found themselves.

One group consisted of the 'Consultants *manqués*': doctors who had hung on for just so long in hospital posts until they could no longer stand the lack of advancement, the constant re-posting and the poor salaries and decided to exchange their dreams for a General Practice where they might settle down comfortably. This was, on the whole, not the sort of person I was looking for. They had worked in hospitals for so long that they no longer understood the very special needs of General Medicine; they had a good understanding of 'cases' but knew little about 'patients', they had advanced treatment at their fingertips but were unaccustomed to carrying with them in a medical bag the thousand and one diagnoses of everyday complaints. They were mainly hard-working, clever – often brilliant – conscientious doctors but they knew little about General Practice, not even how to crack a joke with a patient, and I had little time to train anyone in its particular ways.

The second category of applicants were General Practitioners, the real thing, but with no practices of their own.

Since the advent of the National Health Service had put a stop to the buying and selling of practices, those in popular districts had become increasingly difficult to come by. A glance at the medical journals confirmed the fact that they were crying out for GPs in remote, sparsely populated country districts, but in any sizeable town or pleasant rural practice there were hundreds of applicants for every vacancy. The only alternatives, if one was not lucky enough to land one of these practices, was to put one's plate up or 'squat' in a district that was still open to doctors – at this game one could easily starve in a very short time – or become an assistant or locum to a series of established GPs in the hope of one day being offered a partnership.

It was someone of the second group, well versed in the ways of General Practice, that I hoped to engage and it was with a very real sense of 'there but for the grace' etc. that I interviewed them.

Doctor Frogley soon dispersed the load of compassion I brought to our little discussion and replaced it with a feeling of horror which lasted long after I had shown him the door.

As soon as we had performed the preliminary skirmishes – the removing of hats and coats, the shaking of hands, exchange of pleasantries concerning the district and the weather – and had seated ourselves face to face in armchairs in the morning-room, it became evident that it was Doctor Frogley who was interviewing me.

He was wearing a sports jacket one could best describe, I suppose, as mustard coloured, and with it a green bow-tie. He had a slick moustache on a face which either reflected the tones of his coat or was that way naturally, and grey suede shoes with very pointed toes. He looked as if he would be more at home on a race-track than in a surgery.

"First," he said as soon as he had adjusted the creases in his trousers to his satisfaction and before I had a chance to open my mouth, "What's the salary? Do I get a car allowance and have you got your patients trained?"

"Trained?" I said. "I'm running a practice, not a circus. What exactly do you mean?"

"No visits accepted after ten in the morning, last patient in the waiting-room half an hour before closing time, no injections, no minor surgery, no Saturday mornings – I'm almost down to scratch."

I was curious. Doctor Frogley had sent excellent references from one Doctor Matthews in Birmingham.

"Tell me," I said, "how did Doctor Matthews run his practice?"

Doctor Frogley didn't waste words.

"Surgery open eight a.m., door locked nine-thirty a.m., see first patient ten a.m...."

"Just a minute," I said. "Do I understand that the patients started arriving at eight but that you didn't see anyone until two hours later?"

"Correct! Doctor Matthews believed that the patients should wait upon the doctor and not the doctor upon the patients."

"You mean to say people would just sit there for two hours?"

"Oh, we didn't have any chairs. No room. Didn't get malingerers that way either, just coming in for a chat."

"Then both you and Doctor Matthews started at ten?"

"Correct. Soon polished that little lot off. Minor surgery to Casualty, penicillins to the District Nurse, no speaking unless spoken to, children to be brought in undressed..."

"And the patients stood for all that?"

"Biggest practice in Birmingham," Doctor Frogley said. "All a question of training."

"I'm afraid my patients wouldn't care for those conditions," I said, "and I wouldn't want them to."

"I suppose you do visits all day?" Doctor Frogley asked contemptuously.

"Yes, I do," I admitted, "which is why I need an assistant."

"Gracious, boy," Frogley said, "we had three times as many on our list in Birmingham and never did a call after lunch. We were up at the Club by two."

"Both of you?"

"Both of us. Start as you mean to go on. If you coddle 'em you'll never get a moment's peace. Won't respect you either. Got to run the thing on business lines. Efficiency."

I stood up. "Look," I said, "thank you very much for coming over, Doctor Frogley, but we don't seem to have the same outlook upon this thing. I'm neither running a business nor a cattle farm…"

"I could halve your work in no time…"

"Possibly you could. I prefer to run my practice my way."

"Waste of time. Don't get paid enough for fancy stuff…"

"Perhaps you're right…"

"Of course I'm right…"

"Nevertheless, if you don't mind…"

"All right, boy, all right."

I couldn't stand, more than anything else, being called 'boy'. I handed him his pork-pie and showed him the door.

That there were doctors who ran their practices in this manner I knew, but this was the first time I had actually heard how it was done at first-hand.

The curious thing about it was that there really were people who didn't mind this sort of thing. I could only suppose it was a kind of masochism – the more they suffered the better treatment they received. Any other explanation was quite beyond me. As well as it had seemed to work in the case of Doctors Matthews and Frogley, however, it was an experiment I was unwilling to try.

If anybody could be called the 'opposite' to Doctor Frogley it was Doctor Dibdin. He was as timid as Doctor Frogley was brash; as reticent as Doctor Frogley was verbose.

When I went into the morning-room to conduct the interview I couldn't at first even see him; then I did. He was wearing a fawn suit and he was huddled into a fawn chair in the corner. His hair and his eyebrows toned nicely with his suit. He unfolded himself from the chair and stood eyeing me mournfully, looking, I swear, more like Bambi than any human being I have seen.

"Good morning!" I boomed jovially to put him at his ease. He jumped about a foot in the air.

When he'd recovered from the shock and sat down again so near the edge of the chair I felt sure it was unsafe, I told him, worst things first, what the salary was, and that I was willing to pay a car allowance.

"I'm afraid I don't drive myself," Doctor Dibdin said anxiously and in a voice so soft it was an effort to hear him. "My wife drives me everywhere." I had seen a young woman in a battered Ford outside the house as I came in. I cast a rapid eye up and down the person of Doctor Dibdin but he appeared to have his full complement of arms and legs.

"There's nothing the matter with me," he whispered, interpreting my looks. "It's just my nerves. I used to drive."

"And what happened?"

"I had an accident." He shuddered.

"Fatal?"

He nodded.

"Good Lord," I said. "Did you get charged with manslaughter?"

"Oh, no," he said. "It wasn't a man."

"What then?" I pictured some innocent child lying in the road and my heart hardened against the pathetic Doctor Dibdin.

"It was a chicken," he shuddered again, "it was horrible. You wouldn't believe so much blood..."

"All right," I said, "let's forget about the chicken. Tell me about the locum you've been doing." I referred to the letter he had sent me. "You've been running Doctor Aitken's practice in Luton while he's been ill?"

"That's right."

"Tell me how you organised your day."

"I started the surgery…"

"Do you think you could speak up a bit?"

"That's funny!"

"What?"

"Doctor Aitken was hard of hearing too."

I let it pass. "Carry on," I said.

"I started the surgery at nine…" he hadn't raised his voice a semitone. I leaned forward to catch the words of wisdom. "…and after lunch I did the visits. Then…"

"Just a minute," I stopped him. "Why was it you didn't do any visits before lunch-time?"

He looked surprised. "I told you. I was doing the surgery."

"From nine o'clock?"

He nodded.

"Tell me, Doctor Dibdin, how many people on the average did you see in a morning surgery?"

He thought for a moment. "Six," he said, "normally. Of course when we were busy there'd sometimes be nine or ten."

I sighed. Taking on an assistant was not going to be as easy as I thought.

There were three more after Doctor Dibdin.

Doctor Hunt reeked of whisky; Doctor Gandy wanted too much money; Doctor English looked as if he could do with a bath.

Doctor Killingback, whom I never saw, was the one we frightened away. It was probably my fault as I mistook the time of the appointment. I thought I had said five o'clock and Doctor Killingback had understood four. Unfortunately it was the day of the twins' birthday party and when he arrived Sylvia had popped out to the shops to fetch additional supplies of ice-cream. By the time she returned Doctor Killingback was immobilised in a corner, his legs tied with a skipping-rope, surrounded by a screaming mob of delighted six-year-olds. When she had rescued him, removed the sherbet from his suit, the paper streamer from his hair and the ice-lolly stick from his top pocket, Doctor Killingback remembered quite suddenly an urgent visit he had forgotten to do and made his escape, promising to come back later. To the disappointment of Penny and Peter but not to my surprise, we never saw him again. It was a pity because I liked his name.

That was as far as I got on the day that I went with Sylvia to see the house, and it wasn't very far at all. I could spare her half an hour only, I said, because I had an appointment with Doctor Jaggers on whom I was pinning the tattered shreds of all that remained of my high hopes.

We drove for about ten minutes, Sylvia directing me, towards the Green Belt surroundings of our suburb when I said:

"You realise this house of ours has to be near enough for me to pop back every so often for visits. One has to bear in mind emergencies."

"Turn right," Sylvia said.

I did so.

"Now left, then left again."

We were in a muddy lane.

"Stop."

I stopped. There was nothing to be seen but a hedge, a ditch and a path.

"Sylvia," I said.

She took my arm. "Come on."

She had put her own ankle-boots on but hadn't warned me. By the time we were on the other side of the hedge the mud was well past my turn-ups. I had on one of my newer suits but suddenly I didn't care. On the other side of the hedge was a long, low, white house set into a bowl of green fields.

"Sweetie," I said gently, "are you out of your mind? I'm just a simple GP..." but she was halfway up the drive and couldn't hear a word.

We were shown into a countrified, beautifully proportioned hall by an Italian manservant in a striped waistcoat, and either four or five dogs, I can't be quite sure.

The manservant said *Madama* was with the chickens but wouldn't be long; the dogs sniffed, slobbered and growled.

We sat down in a chintzy, ruggy, photography-room with French windows leading on to a glorious garden, and I looked impatiently at my watch.

Ten minutes later we were still sitting in the chintzy, ruggy room. I opened the French windows and went out into the garden in search of *Madama*. Sylvia, who said I shouldn't go snooping around on my own, stayed where she was.

A path led round the house. I followed it. I crossed a sweep of drive, a small lawn where washing was drying, another path, and then came to an assortment of long, low Nissen-hut arrangements. In the doorway of one of the huts stood what I presumed to be *Madama*. She was wearing a brown felt hat, and had a cigarette hanging from the corner of her mouth.

"Good morning," I said, prepared to be a little snooty with her for keeping us waiting. We had, after all, made an appointment.

"Come on in," she said, holding open the door of the hut. "Just feeding. Hopwood's off sick." Since she had turned her back on me I had no choice but to follow her into the hut. It was long and low and lit with electric light bulbs. Running around on the floor were hundreds and hundreds of chickens.

"Deep litter," she said, turning on me, the cigarette still in her mouth. "Don't believe in all this fancy battery stuff. Simple, plenty of eggs, foolproof."

"How do you mean 'deep litter'?"

"What you're standing on. Leave the droppings. Harden. Generates heat."

I looked at all the flapping, squawking birds.

"What do you do with all the eggs?"

She looked at me as though I was simple. "Sell 'em!"

I followed her out of the chicken-house and along another path to where there were rows of low-built pens.

"Pigs!" she said. "Plenty of profit. No trouble. Breed 'em, fatten 'em, sell 'em."

A fat, purple sow eyed me and snorted adenoidally.

"Mornin' Annabelle!" *Madama* slapped her on the rump affectionately.

I had a sudden vision of myself in gum-boots and a hacking jacket feeding pigs. "What other animals have you?"

"That's all. Pigs and chickens. Plenty of profit. Two cottages in the next field. High rent. Place pays for itself. Keeps me too."

"How many men do you employ?"

"Men? Few bits of birds and a hundred pigs? Just old Hopwood and a boy for the pigs and the general. Chickens are mine."

"Your husband has another occupation then?"

She cackled. "Kicking up the daisies. If you can call it an occupation."

"My brain was ticking over furiously. The smell of the pigs and the chickens had gone to my head.

"So it doesn't take an awful lot of time?" I persisted. "All this?"

"Chickens morning and evening. Your wife could do that. Collect the eggs. Hopwood for the pigs – just a boy if you like – not like cows – looks after itself."

I looked over towards the fields stretching into the distance.

"What about all that stuff?"

She followed my gaze, the cigarette now a stub smouldering at her lips. "Meadows. Rent 'em out for grazing. Free ridin' if you've got kids."

That did it – the thought of Penny and Peter on horseback.

"C'mon," she said: "I'll show you."

When we'd finished our tour and my head was bursting with apple orchards, strawberries (grow themselves), vegetable gardens, ponies, chickens and pigs, we went back into the house. Sylvia said: "I don't mind, Sweetie, I've plenty of time but what about Doctor Jaggers?"

"Good lord!" I said. I had completely forgotten Doctor Jaggers. "Come on!"

"But Sweetie!" Sylvia said. "You haven't even seen the house. The pink bathroom, the walk-in cupboards…"

"Never mind the house. I must get back."

"But that's what we came to see."

"Sweetie," I said; "you understand all about cupboards and things. I'll take your word for it. Let's go."

We thanked *Madama* who said we could come again and look round whenever we liked, and rushed to the car.

After five minutes of dead silence I said:

"Darling, what's the matter? Why aren't you talking to me?"

"I take you all that way," Sylvia wailed, "and you don't even bother to look at it. I don't understand you."

"Angel," I said. "Not only did I look. I thought it was wonderful."

"You did?" She brightened up.

"I can just see myself with those pigs."

"I thought we could rent off the farm bit."

"Darling, that's the best part about it. I've always wanted to work in the open air."

"You aren't contemplating giving up the practice?"

"Of course not. That's the beauty of it. I can combine both. Pigs and chickens take up no time at all."

Sylvia was smiling. "I'm so pleased," she said.

"There's only one snag, of course."

"Yes?"

"We can't possibly afford it!"

I was an hour late for my appointment with Doctor Jaggers. I dropped Sylvia off at the shops and drew up with a screech of brakes outside the house, behind a green Morris Minor. Doctor Jaggers, I presumed, was waiting.

The hall was quiet. I had just taken off my coat and slung it on the banisters when I heard a throaty laugh. It was Caroline's and it came from the morning-room.

I opened the door. Caroline, in leopard-skin pants, was sitting on the lap of a good-looking young man. I had the distinct impression that she was biting his ear but she stopped as I came in.

"Doctor Jaggers?" I said.

The young man lifted Caroline on to the floor and stood up, straightening his tie.

I held out my hand. "I'm sorry I'm late." My voice was heavy with sarcasm.

His hand met mine. "Not at all," he said. "Please don't apologise. Your wife was entertaining me splendidly."

"Doctor Jaggers," I said, he seemed completely to have missed the sarcasm, "Caroline is *not* my wife."

"I understand perfectly," he said, winking a languid eye.

And I found it was I who was blushing.

Eight

Doctor Kirby was the most affable of the lot. He arrived in a green Mercedes, a blue pin-striped suit which I calculated must have cost him at least the equivalent of two weeks of the salary I intended paying him, and hand-made crocodile shoes.

I looked at the letter he had sent me. I think I had asked him to come for an interview out of sheer curiosity. The notepaper was silver grey and as thick as cardboard, the writing enormous, and the ink jet-black.

"How is it, Doctor Kirby," I said, "that you seem to be thirty-six years old and have only been qualified for two years although it says here that you entered St Augustine's to begin your training at the age of eighteen?"

He smoothed back his long hair with a well-kept hand on the little finger of which was a gold signet ring. He was a good-looking fellow.

"I suppose I did mess about a bit actually," he drawled. "Henry was living in Jamaica at the time and I'm a bit of a hedonist myself."

"Henry?"

"The old man. Name's Marchmont actually. Marchmont Calthrop-Kirby."

"Not the timber Calthrop-Kirby?" The man was a millionaire.

"Old 'Woody' himself!"

"Why do you call him Henry?"

"He's had so many wives. Not that he chops off their heads or anything sordid like that. Just wears them out. We're a very virile family."

"I see," I said. "Well, if it's not an impertinent question, what are you doing applying for some poorly paid assistant's post when...?"

"Got to do something," he said. "The old humanity and all that. Not keen on the old parasitic life – not for too long at a stretch at any rate. Between you and me it palls after a time, you know, the cream-filled, mink-iced women, soft as eiderdowns, comfortable of course but frightfully gooey, and those poor pickled goats they drag with them round the world to pay the bills – Panama hats, Bermuda shorts on paunches they never were intended for, cigars on Montego Bay... After a while you feel you can't stand the sight of one more planter's punch. It makes you long for a glimpse of a nice, filthy, hard-worked, festering finger or a whiff of a good old varicose ulcer. You needn't worry that I'm afraid of work or anything. I can put me nose to the grindstone, me shoulder to the wheel and all that, with the best of 'em."

"Good. I'm glad to hear it."

"As for night calls. You needn't worry about those either."

"Why's that?"

"I'll do those for you. I'm at my best at night. I prefer to sleep late in the mornings. I'm an absolute bear until noon. Tell me, Doctor," he took out a black cigarette and stuck it into a gold holder, "what do you intend doing with all your spare time when you have an assistant?"

"As a matter of fact, I'm thinking of getting a small-holding. Just pigs and chickens, you know," I admitted modestly.

"But that's utterly splendid!" He sat forward. "We have a place in Yorkshire, couple of thousand acres only, but I never feel completely at home without a chicken or a pig or two. Battery or deep litter?"

"Deep litter."

"Mm. Inclined to battery myself. With today's market one has to compete. If you really want layers… I'd leave that to you though."

"Thanks," I said. He took no notice.

"I'm more of a pig man meself. Do you know how to choose your sows? Length of body, femininity, well-developed udder, two rows of teats with at least six teats in a row…of course you have to be careful during pregnancy, much of the success of breeding depends on this. People don't realise!"

"I'm sure they don't."

"What about feeding? Hand-feeding? limited-feeding? self-feeding? hogging-down crops?"

"I really don't know. We haven't got the place yet. It's all very much in the air. Look, Doctor Kirby, to get back to business, have you done any Midder?"

"Sure," he said. "It's essential to be accurate about breeding dates and remove them to a clean farrowing pen three days before the birth."

"I was referring to the patients."

He looked blank for a moment then his face cleared. "Yes, the patients," he said despondently. Then, "But I don't suppose they'll bother us too much, will they?"

I was almost ready to abandon the whole project. I said to Sylvia at dinner-time: "Look, darling, I've managed for so many years on my own I can carry on for a bit longer. I can't stand seeing any more of these chaps. One knows almost from the 'Off' whether they're going to be any use or not, yet you still have to go through with the whole rigmarole as though you were really interested. I haven't the time to waste. Besides, none of them are suitable. I suppose if they were any good most of them would have settled down long ago."

Then Caroline came in. She was wearing what looked like black woollen combs which covered her from neck to ankle so tightly that they looked positively obscene. She struck a pose in the doorway.

"Doc!" she said dramatically. "I've great news."

"Yes."

"Little old Caroline has found him."

"Found who?"

"Whom. The assistant!"

"Not again!" I said, remembering her amorous entanglement with Doctor Jaggers. "Anyway where is he?"

"He called while you were in surgery and Sylvia was bathing the kids." She looked at her watch. "I told him to come round at eight-thirty. And if he's not what you're looking for I'll jump off the Empire State."

"What's his name?"

"Doctor Curit."

"He must be a phoney!"

"He's the goods, Doc. I'll swear to it."

"Tell me exactly what happened."

"He called and said he was after the assistant's situation. I told him you were tied up with a patient just then and he said not to trouble putting the call through. So I asked him a few pertinent questions..."

"Such as?"

"Where he'd qualified, how many internships he'd done, previous experience, whether his grandparents were living and if not what they died of..."

"What's that got to do with it?"

"Heredity. Very important in character assessment."

"And he answered all those questions on the telephone?"

"Sure. That's how keen he was. Answered up smartly too. Good voice; businesslike, to the point..."

"OK." I was already catching Caroline's terminology. "I'll have a look at him if he turns up."

"He'll turn up all right." She looked at me. "You mean you think I scared him?"

I looked at my watch. "It's now eight-twenty-eight. In approximately two minutes we shall know."

Caroline moved towards the table.

"You aren't going to have dinner in that thing?" I pointed at her clinging garment through which every muscle and protrusion was emphasised. "What's it supposed to be?"

Caroline, unperturbed, took her place at the table swinging one long black leg over the other.

"Never seen a leotard, Doc? You just ain't educated."

Caroline had just finished her tomato juice and started on the grilled grapefruit which was her main dish for the evening meal when the bell rang. She made an 'I told you so!' face at me.

"You'd better let him in," I said, "considering he's your find."

She stood up, the outlines of her shapely behind accentuated by the skin-tightness of the leotard thing.

"On second thoughts," I said, remembering Doctor Jaggers, "I'd better let him in myself."

"Aw, Doc!" she said repoachfully, "you're getting awful stuffy!" and was gone out of the door.

After five minutes, when Caroline hadn't returned, Sylvia said:

"You'd better go. Although, knowing that cousin of yours, it's probably too late. She's most likely eaten him alive."

So I finished my steak and went into the morning-room to interview the estimable Doctor Curit.

He was standing with his back to me reading a copy of the *Medical Journal*. Caroline was curled up on the sofa staring at him like a far-gone sex-symbol on a film poster.

Doctor Curit turned round.

"Faraday!" I said. "You bastard."

He shook my hand. "I've very good qualifications," he said. "That's if you're not suited."

"How did you know I was looking for someone?"

"Read the ad.," he indicated the journal. "Just got back from Switzerland." He looked at Caroline and raised an eyebrow. "Where's Sylvia?"

"Inside. This is my cousin Caroline from the States. She's staying with us."

"Not Uncle Arthur's? The freckly brat with the pigtails?"

"The very same. Caroline, be a dear and tell Sylvia Faraday's here."

Caroline unwound herself like a black panther from the sofa. As she undulated past Faraday she said: "Doctor Curit! Louse!" And war was declared.

It was typical of Faraday to have pretended to be applying for the assistant's job. The years had neither sobered down his boyishness nor robbed him of his medical student brand of humour. His lately acquired consultant status seemed not to have affected him.

"Congratulations, darling!" Sylvia said when she came in and she and Faraday flung their arms round each other.

"All right, break it up," I said.

Faraday released Sylvia.

"No nice girls in Switzerland?" I said.

"Plenty – they all wanted to stay there."

"Well, you can't possibly be a Harley Street Consultant without a large studio portrait of your wife on your desk. It's bad for business."

"Couldn't we share Sylvia?"

"No, we could not!"

"I mean the photograph, of course."

I glared at him.

"It would look frightfully impressive."

"No doubt."

"When do you start in private practice?" I said, to change the subject.

"I've started. Number 266 Harley Street. Telephone number Wimpole 3833. Kindly make a note and for pity's sake send me

83

some patients." He took a large white envelope out of his pocket, removed some square white tickets and handed them to me. "This is what I really came for."

They were tickets for a Medical Dinner and Dance.

"Decent of you," I said. "Are you taking us?"

"Like hell. I thought you might take me. I shall have to circulate now. Ingratiate myself with the GPs and their wives, of course." He put his arms round Sylvia.

"You needn't start on Sylvia. I shall send you some patients without that."

"I was practising."

"Knowing you, you don't need any practice."

"Ingratiating yourself at a dance is not enough," Sylvia said. "You have to entertain the GPs and their wives. Dinner, cocktails, that sort of thing. We're always being asked."

"Baked-beans on toast, sitting on the bed, in Earls Court?" Faraday said. He cocked an eye at Sylvia. "Unless, of course…"

"No, you may not borrow Sylvia," I said. "There must be a girl somewhere."

"For what?" a voice from the doorway said. And Caroline was standing draped against the jamb pointing a deprecating finger at Faraday.

"What about Caroline?" I said, "she's a nice girl. Easy to get on with, healthy – well, almost."

"Sweet of you, Doc," Caroline said. "I don't happen to have the mating urge right now."

"Give me a tinkle," Faraday said, his face straight, "when you have."

We arranged to go with Faraday to the Medical Dance so that he could mingle with the possible future sources of his bread and butter, and spent the rest of the evening talking shop. It was a pastime I enjoyed greatly. When he was talking medicine Faraday was a changed man. Gone was the flippancy, the light word, the smart answer. Medicine was the love of his life, his work, his hobby, the keeper of his thoughts waking and sleeping. I often discussed my less straightforward cases with him and he usually managed to shed new and serious light on the subject.

Before we realised, it was midnight. Sylvia and Caroline had long ago said good night and gone to bed.

I walked up the path with Faraday. It was a cold, bright night.

"How does it feel?" I said as he got into his ancient car, "to have made the grade?"

"Tremendous," he said. "I feel it's the start of great things."

"I hope it is," I said. "Well, see you at the dance. We'll bring Caroline."

Faraday dismissed her with a wave of the hand. "Send patients," he said. "More important."

He pulled the starter and to the accompaniment of a horrible grating noise which must have annoyed a few of the neighbours was off down the road.

Things happen in unexpected ways and in unexpected places.

I found my new assistant at three o'clock next morning in a pub.

Mrs Weaver, wife of the licensee was in labour with her fourth. She was one of my old faithfuls who had moved out of the district, where she and her husband had once run the Three Feathers, and I now looked after her at the Wooden Whistle in town.

It took me almost forty minutes to get there.

When I arrived a young man in a dressing-gown with his sleeves rolled up was leaning over the bed with his ear to her abdomen.

"I'm not too sure about the foetal heart and I think she's second staging," he said amiably.

"Who are you?"

He put his hands in his dressing-gown pocket. "Letchworth's the name. Doctor Robin Letchworth. I'm staying the night here and Mr Weaver called me while you were in transit. Not that I could do much, I've no equipment, but there was a bit of a panic all round."

He watched me unpack my things. Mrs Weaver was groaning.

"Can I give you a hand? I'm a bit of a dab at Midder?"

Mrs Weaver screamed. Things seemed to be moving rapidly.

"Perhaps it would be a good idea," I said, and threw him a mask. "Hang on to her leg for me, will you." With myself conducting, Mrs Weaver as the Prima Donna and Robin Letchworth as the first violin, our little trio took an hour to produce a nine-pound baby boy.

During the recital, the chief burden, as always, being borne by the Diva, I learned that Robin Letchworth had come to London from Scotland, where he had been helping in a large practice, with an idea of looking for an assistantship with a possible view. He was unmarried, accustomed to the ways of General Practice, on the Midder list and keen.

By the time the last act was over and the chief performer had been suitably rewarded, in her arms a child, not roses, I had engaged my new assistant.

We drank to our alliance and the health of the latest little Weaver in the Wooden Whistle's best champagne uncorked by the proud father.

Robin was free to start work on the following Monday.

It was as simple as that.

Nine

It takes so little to change one's perspective. A woman sees a dress in a shop window. The price is more than she can afford but in her imagination the dress does something magical for her, transforms her. She broods, waits, dreams, hopes, talks softly to her husband and finally buys it. It costs ten, twenty, thirty or forty pounds. She covers it with a dust-cover, clears a space for it in the wardrobe, buys accessories to go with it and, on very special occasions wears it. It is dark, calf length and waisted. It is her pride and joy. Three months later fashion decrees that dresses shall be pale, loose from shoulder to hip and barely cover the knee. The lady opens her wardrobe. What a moment ago had been her pride and joy is barely two yards of not very expensive material stitched together into an unfashionable shape. It is no longer smart enough for best and is too dressy for every day. The dust-cover is removed. The dress, crammed together with others, is a liability; it is endured – it was, after all, expensive – worn occasionally, finally hated. When the old-clothes man comes with his five shillings, she wonders how she could ever have been so criminally extravagant as to pay more for the meaningless lump of stuff. The following day she sees a dress in a shop window; it is pale, waistless and barely covers the knee…

With me it wasn't, of course, a dress. It was my new assistant (due shortly to start work), our new house (which we wanted desperately but couldn't hope to be able to afford), Cousin

Caroline and numerous domestic and medical problems that in the course of a few hours vanished, as though they had never been, from my mind, changing from problems of such magnitude that one or other of them occupied my thoughts waking and sleeping, to a collection of trivia so unimportant that when temporarily cast aside I did not even notice the loss.

I suppose it is in the order of things that events occasionally happen to shake up the kaleidoscope of images we carry around and resettle them in a different light. One wonders sometimes if such drastic measures are always necessary in order merely to change the pattern.

Wednesday, bright but with a cold east wind, began with no prodromal or warning symptoms.

I was in a particularly good mood. Having settled the problem of an assistant I could hardly wait until the following Monday when he was due to begin. Some peculiar rumours of the forthcoming changes had apparently been circulating in the practice.

One lady, a regular Wednesday morning attender since I had first started in the practice had sat firmly before me on Tuesday and said: "I come today because I heard you was retirin'."

"Retiring? Whatever made you think that?"

"That's what they're saying."

"Well, you can tell 'them' from me that I'm doing no such thing. I'm *expanding* my practice, in fact, with the help of an assistant."

"Oh." She looked unconvinced. "Well, I thought I'd better come today, seein'."

Another, an elderly Irishman, said: "I'm surprised yer still here, Doctor!"

"Oh? Where am I supposed to be going?"

"A world cruise, isn't it?"

It sounded good. I sighed and disillusioned him.

Little Mrs Lane said: "May I offer you my congratulations, Doctor," and held out her hand.

I shook the hand.

"How much was it?" she said.

"How much?"

"I heard you won the pools."

"I'm sorry, Mrs Lane," I said. "I wish I had."

They said they were sorry to lose me, that they had now grown used to me, that I would be missed. In spite of the fact that I had no intention of going anywhere I was touched.

On this particular morning I rushed happily into my surgery, twenty minutes late because of Baby Waites' broncho-pneumonia, to find Penny and Peter sitting sedately on the two chairs that faced my desk.

The twins were as neurotic and introspective a pair of kids as one could find anywhere and I put the condition down to the influence of their environment.

I had the telephone on the table at meal-times. If a patient rang for advice while we were eating, the twins invariably listened intently to my side of the conversation and when I had replaced the receiver they always wanted to know exactly what kind of foreign body had been swallowed, put in the ear or pushed up the nose (in the case of beads they had to know the colour too), from where the blood was coming, if it was a case of haemorrhage, or exactly which part of the body was not functioning. Usually two or three days later they managed to reproduce these second-hand symptoms in themselves. Penny had admitted many times to severe headache, stomach ache (accompanied by rolling eyes) and total incapacity to move various limbs, while Peter had announced one day with all solemnity that he was about to have a baby. No day passed without various sores, scabs and scratches, usually so minute they were barely visible, being presented at the most inopportune moments for my inspection, and I had now made a ruling that all complaints could only be dealt with in the surgery.

They had apparently taken me at my word.

"Look, children," I said, one hand on the buzzer which would summon the first patient from the waiting-room, "I've no time now to talk to you and if you don't hurry you'll be late for school. Mummy's waiting."

"But, Daddy," Penny said, looking hurt, "you *said* in the surgery."

"I know." I could see they were determined. "All right. I'll give you two and a half minutes and that's more than most people get at the moment. What's the trouble?"

"It's Peter," Penny said. "He's got a spot."

"Where?"

She turned maternally to Peter who was sitting on his chair looking pious. "Show him, Peter." She tugged vaguely at his pullover which Peter started to remove.

"Just tell me where it is, there's a good chap. I'll do the undressing."

"On my back."

I whipped his pullover, shirt and vest up to his shoulders and peered at the smooth flesh.

"I can't see anything."

Penny stood up and leaned over him. "There!" she said, pointing a triumphant finger.

I looked closer. With my eyes about an inch away I could just distinguish a dot of red no larger than the proverbial pin-head.

"Oh," I said and went back to the desk. "That's nothing to worry about."

"It iches," Peter said hopefully.

"It'll stop."

"Don't I need to put anything on it?"

"No. It'll go away."

Penny stood up. "You gave Michael some stuff in a chube when he had spots," she said.

I sighed. "Michael had impetigo."

Suddenly I came to my senses and wondered why I was standing there arguing with my own children.

"Now come along," I said severely, "that's enough. There are people queueing down the path. Go and get ready for school this minute."

They recognised the voice of authority and left, Peter with his vest hanging out.

It was eleven-thirty before I finished the surgery and I had a list of visits to do as long as any I had ever had. As I slammed the front door behind me it was immediately opened again.

"Doc!" Caroline was standing there in tight black skirt, very high-heeled shoes and nylon bra. On her head was a hat like a pink beehive.

"Can you drop me off at the station? I'm awful late."

"Like that?"

"I'll be three minutes. I just have to curl my eyelashes."

"Look, Caroline, I've no time to hang around this morning. I've more visits than I can manage and anyway I'm not going past the station. I'm going in the opposite direction."

She pouted. "I've an important engagement."

"Well, you should have got ready earlier."

"I did. My zipper stuck."

"Look, Caroline…"

"It is in the interests of Sex!" she pleaded.

It was quicker not to argue.

"I'll call back in five minutes," I said. "If you aren't on the kerb ready to jump in you've had it!"

"Doc," she breathed, "you're a real gent."

Half an hour later I was palpating Mrs Stranaghan's abdomen when I suddenly remembered Caroline.

"Oh no!" I said.

Mrs Stranaghan sat up. "It's something serious!"

I reassured her, prescribed for her gastritis, and turned the car round towards home.

Caroline, a kind of orange-coloured tent now flowing beneath her pink beehive, had spread a newspaper on the kerb and was sitting on it.

"You'll be had up for vagrancy," I said as she got into the car.

"And you'll be scalped for letting me sit on the sidewalk for twenty-five minutes like a tramp," she said, never at a loss for an answer.

I was unrepentant. "You shouldn't interrupt my work. I don't run a taxi service."

She opened her mouth.

"And I don't care if it is in the interests of Sex!" I said.

"I have a very important conference."

"Who with?"

"A Miss Entwhistle and a Mr Tree."

"Where?"

"Mile End."

"Do you know where that is?"

"East Side," she said.

"That's a slum area."

"Sure! I'm not a snob."

I looked at her in her crazy hat and winkle-picker shoes. "You can't go down there dressed like that!"

She bridled. "I'm an ambassador of my country."

"I hope the natives respect your diplomatic immunity," I said, and at that moment we heard the first fire-engine coming up behind us fast.

I pulled in to the kerb to allow it to pass and Caroline sat bolt upright, her eyes shining with excitement.

"Go on," she said. "What are we waiting for?"

"I'm not waiting for anything."

"Well, let's get after it. Isn't it exciting?"

Another engine, bells ringing wildly, clanged past us.

"Caroline," I said, "don't be morbid. Another day I'll take you to a fire with pleasure, but I happen to be in the middle of a busy morning. Anyway what about Miss Entwhistle?"

But Caroline was gazing after the fire-engine entranced.

"Ever since I was a kid," she said, "fire-engines have done something for me."

"Perhaps that accounts for everything," I said, but my words were lost in the noise of the third scarlet engine passing us urgently and at speed.

"C'mon!" Caroline yelled, waving her arm, and her enthusiasm was infectious.

I put my foot on the accelerator and followed dangerously close in the wake of the engine.

We could smell the smoke almost immediately.

"It can't be very far off," Caroline said, leaning out of the window and clutching the pink beehive on her head.

At the same moment as I saw an orange flame leap up above the houses, snatch at the colourless sky and then receded again, I was aware of a peculiar and unfamiliar sensation in my entrails. The fire-engine in front of me turned two more corners so fast I thought it must turn over, then pulled up so suddenly that Caroline and I almost went through the windscreen.

I couldn't move for what seemed an eternity but could only have been seconds. We were in a quiet side street before a large building half of which was burning furiously. There were screams, shouts, people running, firemen, ambulances.

"Some fire!" Caroline said, and then she followed my horrified eyes to the sign which read: 'Bushfield Park Primary School'.

I don't remember getting out of the car but have just a vision of Caroline running along the pavement and across the playground beside me in her stockinged feet, her long hair flowing behind her, as she pulled off the beehive hat.

It seemed that one-half of the school only was ablaze; the section above the boiler-rooms. From the other section frightened children were filing into the playground. Inside the building, bells still sounded the alarm.

Firemen, teachers, policemen, passers-by from the street, pushed through the corridors against the flow of children, coughing and spluttering as they pressed nearer the heart of the fire. My eyes flicked each child for a moment.

"Penny and Peter," I was saying continuously and probably aloud, "Penny and Peter."

I saw little Philip Bradshaw, Ronnie Smith from down the road, Jennifer Hardy trotting seriously behind the teacher.

There were others behind me. As we passed down the corridors we looked quickly into each classroom the children had vacated to make sure no one had been left behind.

In the Art Class a small girl in a pinafore was unbelievably standing before her easel sloshing poster colours on to the grey paper before her.

"I just been excused," she explained and looked quite hurt when she was picked up by a strong arm and hustled outside.

A woman was shouting "Myra! Myra!" and someone said: "...the trouble is that it happened during playtime and they are all over the school."

We found a small boy standing wide-eyed at the entrance to the cloakroom from which smoke was pouring forth.

"I left my biscuit in my blazer," he kept saying, "I left my biscuit in my blazer": then he too was swept off his feet.

We tied handkerchiefs round our faces but even so it was impossible to go down the steps into the playground again to approach the cloakrooms from the outside entrance where we left the children every morning.

The children were now standing in neat lines in the playground and teachers were counting heads.

I saw Miss Woodcock's class, in which the twins were, huddled along the fence. It took a moment for my eyes to sweep along the line. There was no one looking after them and no Penny and Peter. A teacher with red hair was counting the line next to them.

"Where's Miss Woodcock?" I said.

The teacher looked distractedly towards an ambulance pulling out of the gate.

"She was on cloakroom duty," she said and turned back to her task.

"Have you seen Penny and Peter?" I addressed Class Two A in general.

In the manner of six-year-olds they stared at me.

"They were here before," a fat child standing on one leg said helpfully.

"Before what?" I was agonising. I could hear timber crackling.

"Before." He changed over legs.

"Before playtime?"

He nodded.

I ran towards the cloakroom entrance before which a circle of firemen stood playing their hoses.

Behind me I heard the voice of the Headmistress call: "Everyone, after me, into the street, March!"

They had a ladder up at the top windows. A fireman was climbing down with a boy of ten or eleven over his shoulder. Another ambulance, its doors open, was backing up to take the place of the one that had sped off with Miss Woodcock.

Caroline appeared from a side entrance carrying a child wrapped in her orange tent coat. Her face was black. She laid the child into a pair of outstretched arms then turned back the way she had come.

"You can't go in there, Miss," one of the firemen called. "The beams is going." But Caroline had already disappeared.

Across the playground the woman was running still calling for Myra.

It was getting too hot almost to stand there. The screaming, the shouting, the noise, the smell, the smoke and the flames were like a nightmare. The entire district seemed to have arrived. My thoughts were unfaceable. It would be typical of Penny and Peter to have been up to some scheme in the cloakrooms at playtime. I soaked my handkerchief in water from one of the fire-buckets and decided to go in at the side, the way Caroline had gone, to look for them. Just then the fireman came down the ladder again, dripping with water, holding a small child he had found in an upstairs corridor, overcome by fumes. There was no ambulance there at that moment.

I was on my way to the side entrance feeling as sick as I ever had when a voice screamed.

"Doctor! Please!" and it was Mrs Lindsay from our road and the unconscious child was hers.

I ran after the fireman who had been on the ladder but he shook his head: "There's no more kiddies in there, Sir. This is the last on 'em."

"But my twins," I said, "they weren't with their class…"

There was a great shout of "Stand back, everybody! Stand well back!" and the Fire Brigade Captain was looking anxiously up at the burning part of the building.

I kneeled on the asphalt by little Margaret Lindsay.

By the time she had regained consciousness and another ambulance had arrived it was too late for anyone to go back into what was now a fiery furnace with any hope of survival.

A policeman who had lost his helmet restrained the distracted mother, still calling for 'Myra', from hurling herself suicidally into the flames and the Headmistress came running red-faced from the street and said: "We're missing two!" Then she saw me.

I waited among a gradually dwindling crowd for three hours I would never care to endure again.

They stopped the fire spreading but of half the building only one wall remained. It smoked and dripped. The firemen pulled the hoses like snakes across the ground back on to the engines. Bulging-pocketed reporters arrived from the local newspaper; they took the janitor away half-crazy – it was his boilers that had burst causing the fire; they found Myra cowering in a cupboard in the unburned part of the building.

Of Penny and Peter there was not a sign and I had no idea what had happened to Caroline.

I know I answered countless questions put to me by patient police officers. They wrote my answers down laboriously in little books.

When they'd finished with me I went home.

All I remember of the journey back was that I ran over something pink in the road. Days afterwards I realised that it must have been Caroline's beehive hat. I'd lost count of time but I knew it was late and that Sylvia must be wondering what had kept me. Was it possible to tell her?

Everyone has moments in his life which seem impossible to bear. This was mine. My hands were trembling too much to put the key in the lock, and sweat was creeping coldly down my back. I rang the bell.

Sylvia opened the door, frowning with anxiety. "It's half past three..." she said, then stopped, I suppose, at the sight of my face.

There was a noise behind her like a herd of rhinoceroses falling down the stairs and it was the most wonderful sound I had ever heard in my life.

Penny and Peter flung themselves into my arms.

"We've got the chicking-pops, we've got the chicking-pops!" they chanted. From the recesses of my memory I recalled Peter showing me a spot on his back...

They stopped dancing up and down.

Penny said: "We're ill."

"Chicking-pops!" Peter said importantly and pointed at his sister. "Look at her face. And I've got three."

"Miss Woodcock sent us home."

"She said we shouldn't have come to school at all."

I went down on my knees and hugged them both.

"Daddy!" Peter screamed. "You'll catch some."

"Sylvia," I said, remembering. "Where's Caroline?"

"Out. She's out for the day, she said…" I followed her glance towards the front door which I had left open. Through it, soundlessly in bare feet, crept Caroline.

We all stared. Her clothes were torn, her face was streaked with black, she had a scarf, tied like a washer-woman round her head.

"I went home with a child," she whispered. "They brought me back."

It seemed as much as she could do to raise an arm and pull the scarf, which she must have borrowed, it didn't look like Caroline, from her head. She straightened up a little and stood staring at us almost defiantly.

Penny was the first to recover.

"Look, Peter," she shrieked, "Cousin Caroline's lost her hair!"

And indeed she had.

Like a collaborator she stood there, grimy faced and as bald as a coot. What did one say?

Perhaps it was fortunate at that moment she collapsed, like an ugly rag-doll on the floor.

Ten

Like a machine that had stopped it took us quite a while to warm up and get going again at our customary rate. Even the twins were subdued but then they were, of course, ill, Peter quite severely, with chicken-pox.

Like most doctors, I was quite unable to cope with illness in my own children. I don't mean just Peter's solitary spot to which I failed to give a name on that ghastly Wednesday, although had I really been paying attention, as I would have done with a patient, I would have examined him properly for further evidence and at least suspected chicken-pox, as every other child in the neighbourhood had it, and kept the twins home from school.

Whenever I was called in to see a child patient, I would enter the sick-room confidently, take the history from the mother, examine the child, screaming or not, arrive at a positive diagnosis and prescribe accordingly.

Not so with Penny and Peter. I suppose when it is one's own children the emotional factor has to be reckoned with and that it was this that led me either to stand there like a dithering idiot unable to reach any conclusion when one of them was ill, or else to see every sore throat, headache or stomach pain as incipient diptheria, brain tumour or appendicitis. This blind spot had led me to call upon, on numerous occasions, any of my friends who happened to be paediatricians, neurologists or surgeons for assistance with my own small family. None of them minded coming the least bit and they all assured me, as I rather shamefacedly apologised for bothering them, that my short-comings was one common to all GPs with young families.

When the children were ill Sylvia was really more helpful than I. "I'm sure they just ate too much trifle at the party today," she'd say cheerfully while Penny and Peter vomited in the small hours of the morning. I'd nod dumbly in agreement but all the while my head would be spinning with the preliminary symptoms of acute encephalitis, of which vomiting was one, or the early signs of overwhelming, generalised peritonitis.

And so it happened that at the ripe old age of six Penny and Peter were accustomed to being examined by specialists in whatever complaint they had. They took a morbid interest in their own pathology and submitted with grave attention to any blood test, questioning or examination to which they were put. At the sight of a spatula they would open their mouths wide enough to admit a clenched fist; at the rattle of a hypodermic they would bare their behinds, and one had only to remove the auroscope from its box to find them presenting one or other ear for inspection.

During the course of the illness they now had, they asked me every morning and evening with monotonous regularity, whether I didn't think it advisable to call in a 'chicking-pops' specialist. It was clear when I assured them I was quite capable of dealing unaided with this particular complaint that they had not very much faith in my healing powers, particularly as Peter was in quite a bad way.

We were quite a household of invalids. The twins were in bed with their chicken-pox in one room and Caroline recovering from the effects of the fire in another.

'Bushfield Park Primary School' had escaped lightly. Although half the building no longer existed, there had been no loss of life.

The worst casualty had been poor Miss Woodcock whose misfortune it had been to be on duty in the cloakroom at the time when the explosion in the boiler-room occurred, and almost as badly burned was the small Webster child whose life Caroline had undoubtedly saved.

I had visited them both in the local hospital. Miss Woodcock, although the extent of her burns was very little less than that from which it was not possible to make a recovery, spoke of how thankful she was that all the children had been saved, and from her pain, which must have been very great, she even managed to enquire for Penny and Peter.

One or two of the children, slightly burned or merely suffering from the effects of smoke and fumes, had been discharged from hospital after a couple of days. Little Beryl Webster remained, flat on her back, arms and legs covered with tulle gras, in the children's ward. It would be a long, long time before she would be running around again. Had it not been for Caroline she would not have survived at all. Caroline had found her in one of the toilets, overcome by fumes. Although the part of the cloakroom, through which one had to pass to reach the toilets, had been half ablaze, Caroline had, she said, a premonition that a child still remained in one of the cubicles beyond. She had managed to reach little Beryl safely but when she turned to get back the entire room seemed to be alight. She had put the child under her arm and decided that the only way she had any chance of getting out was to dash as fast as she could between the flames, which had caught two sets of coat rails, and hope for the best. So she had dashed and reached the other side in safety, unaware that her own long hair was alight. A fireman, entering the cloakroom from the opposite direction had promptly smothered her head in his jacket and, saving her life although not her hair, led her and the child to safety.

Now she was suffering from the effects of shock rather than anything else although her forehead and one arm were slightly burned.

You had to admire her. Nine women out of ten, suffering such a disfiguring loss as Caroline had, would have put themselves in purdah. Not so Caroline. She swathed her head in endless variations of tulle and ribbon which she sat in bed sewing, and invited the whole world into her bedroom. She was lucky enough to have one of those faces which could stand on its own without the softening effects of a head of hair but even so it was difficult to look her in the eye. Caroline, however, gay as always, put everyone at his ease. Whenever we went to see her she requested that we admire her latest outrageous headgear, chattered on about all the Sex she was missing during her enforced stay in bed, and told us all how much she was longing to get out again so that she would be able to buy a really sensational, strawberry blonde wig. It had always been her ambition, or so she said, both to wear a wig and be a strawberry blonde; now the opportunity for both had come. She laughed, sang, sent gifts in from her own sick-bed to the twins, and acted the fool in general. I thought there was no getting her down, until one afternoon I went to her room when she wasn't expecting anyone.

After lunch Caroline had informed us all that she was going to sleep and wasn't to be disturbed until four when she would delight us all with an entirely new line in headwear that she had spent the morning making.

At three o'clock, while doing some work with my microscope I discovered the need for a box of slides I had collected during my student days. Sylvia said she'd put them all away, together with my articulated jaw and pickled foetus in the top cupboard in the spare bedroom.

"You can't go up now," she said, "Caroline's asleep."

"I have to have it," I said. "I'll creep. I shan't disturb Caroline."

And so I crept, making no noise at all, into the spare bedroom which Caroline had now made her own.

Caroline wasn't asleep. She was out of bed, sitting before the dressing-table mirror and staring at her bald head, on which already there was a faint grey-looking stubble. Tears were falling slowly down her face.

"Caroline," I said, because for the moment I could think of nothing else.

But all she did was to stare at her grotesque image and say: "My God! My God!"

I felt like a criminal. This was her private moment and I had intruded. My first reaction was to slip out again pretending that I had seen nothing but then I thought, after all she's only a kid for all her sophistication, miles from home, and decided I had better stay.

I sat on the dressing-stool next to her and put my arm round her. For a moment she just continued staring into the mirror, then she collapsed with her head on my shoulder and sobbed as though she would never stop.

I told her how brave she had been; that if it hadn't been for her the child would have perished in the fire; that her hair would soon grow; that she looked beautiful anyway; that we all loved her; that I would buy her a wig; that the most fashionable women wore wigs now anyway; that she had strength of character which was far more important than a few tufts of hair; that we would look after her.

Eventually the sobs came at longer intervals. When she finally raised her head and looked at her swollen face and red eyes, even I had to admit that she didn't look too good.

"Now I've done it properly!" she said. But as she spoke the corners of her mouth lifted in a smile and I caught a glimpse of the old Caroline we all knew and had taken for granted. I should have guessed that a lot of it was bravado.

She got back into bed and I sat beside her and we had a long talk.

She told me why she had left home and come to England. It wasn't really for her Sociology studies at all. They were merely the excuse.

There had been a man, she said, the most wonderful man who ever breathed, or at least so she had thought. He was older than she, thirty-five in fact, tall, dark and handsome. It had been love at first sight. From the first moment they had walked, talked and thought in step, and loved each other dearly. There was only one ripple on the pond of their happiness. The man was married. Of course, his wife didn't understand him. He promised Caroline that he was in the process of divorcing her and that in three months at the most he would be free to marry her. The three months at the most turned into six and the six into a year. After two years, the wife whistled and the man, with apologies to Caroline, went back to her. Caroline, heart-broken at his perfidy, having been convinced he was as much in love with her as she had been and still was, with him, had come to England to forget.

"I'm sorry," I said when she'd finished. "I would never have imagined."

"Why should you? It's purely personal."

"And are you getting over it?"

"Times I think so. I keep telling myself I was young and stupid." She sighed. "Sometimes I'm awful hard to convince." She picked up a wallet from the side of her bed and showed me his photograph. From the expression on her face I could see that she hadn't got over it at all.

He was good-looking enough in a Marlon Brandoish way. He had his arm round her and she was laughing up at him with adoration.

"Jones Beach," she said. "Last Fall."

She put the wallet back again.

"Don't worry about me, Doc," she said, almost in her old, cheerful way. "I'm the kinda girl that needs plenty of lovin' and you don't get much change from a snapshot."

"We'll have to see what we can do for you," I said but she shook her head.

"Ugh-ugh. I prefer to do my own dirty work. It takes me a long time to fall but when the penny drops I know at once. When you hear the click you'll know I've gone."

"I shall listen carefully," I said.

Caroline glanced at her bedside clock. "Doc, would you do something for me?"

"Of course."

"On the chest you'll see a dark blue bottle. In it there's an astringent lotion with the same pH as tears and just what the doctor ordered for weepy eyes. Could you soak two pads of cotton with it and hand it over here?"

I did as she asked and she closed her eyes and laid the two pads over them, like a woman under treatment in a beauty parlour.

"Thirty minutes," she said, "and I'll be a new woman. It says so on the bottle; in French."

"I'll just get what I came in for then and leave you."

"Okey-dokey. Doc?"

"Yes?"

"I really have let my hair down, haven't I?"

I was glad she couldn't see my face.

"No one has to know, do they?"

"Not a soul," I promised. "Try to sleep."

At midnight when I came in from a visit to Mrs MacConnal who this time had had an exceedingly severe attack of cardiac-asthma, I found Sylvia curled up and asleep in an armchair in the morning-room. She looked exhausted and it wasn't surprising; the last few days had been harder for her than they had for me. She had three invalids to look after as well as the usual cooking, washing, ironing and telephone answering for we were between 'helps'. She opened her eyes as I put my case down and I watched her weary attempt to orientate herself.

"Poor Sweetie," I said.

"Thank heavens it's not morning. I had a horrible feeling it was time to get up."

"Why didn't you go to bed?"

"Too tired to get undressed."

"No more calls, are there?"

She looked at the message pad on the arm of her chair. "The midwife to say that Mrs Heap had her baby. She was only in labour for twenty minutes so there was no time to call you."

Thank heavens for small mercies.

Sylvia sat up now properly awake. "I suppose you couldn't go down to Victoria Station tomorrow evening at five-thirty?"

"Anything else? Why?"

"I had a letter from Miss Winterhalter."

"Who's she?"

"Our new *au pair*."

She took the letter from her handbag and unfolded it. "She comes 'with the train and then with another train and then with the boat and then with the train again and will we please hold her from the station'."

"Where's she coming from?"

"Switzerland."

"Well, I certainly can't unless I cancel the evening surgery."

"She also sends 'many greets'."

"Good. I hope she knows how to wash-up."

"She'll soon learn in this house. Who shall I get to 'hold' her from the station?"

"You'd better ring Straker in the morning. Give him a photograph of her and he'll sort it out."

Straker was a patient of mine who ran a car-hire service in the district.

"I shan't be sorry to see her," Sylvia said.

"Miss Winterhalter *and* Doctor Letchworth. This is no life," I said.

"How was Mrs MacConnal?"

"Bed. Two or three more attacks and I reckon she'll have had it."

"What did she have to say today?"

"Nothing. She was too ill. Her husband accused me of giving her inferior treatment because they didn't live in 'one o' them swank houses up on the Mount'."

"Cheek!"

"He was drunk. Don't worry, Sweetie; one day I shall be appreciated even if it's only in the Obituary columns of the *BMJ*. It'll be one of those short paragraphs right at the end of the announcements. After the MD 'well known for his work on the control and prevention of tuberculosis for which he received a knighthood in nineteen o four', complete with photograph, of course (coronary thrombosis – two columns); after the 'Senior General Surgeon in the Brighton and Lewes and Mid-Sussex hospital groups' (died in his sleep – one column); after the 'Consultant Radiologist to the Leeds groups' ('following a short illness' – half a column); after the FRCS 'for many years a well known gynaecologist in Birmingham (good temper and ready smile always in evidence); after the older GPs formerly in practice in Bantham, Deven or Ashton-under-Lyne, you'll find a few lines written by a colleague of mine only too happy to grab my patients... I quote: '...he was a Trojan for work, and I often marvelled how he found time with his busy practice and many confinements to enjoy his hobbies of stamp-collecting and bee-keeping...' "

"You mean golf," Sylvia said.

"Don't interrupt. '...a much esteemed colleague, his breezy humour and confident manner acted as a tonic to an anxious patient and inspired confidence in a worried patient. No trouble was ever too much for him where the interests of the sick were concerned.' "

"Huh!" Sylvia said.

" '...by his death in the flower of his youth the profession and district where he practised have lost a doctor who still cherished the ideals of the fast-disappearing older generation but was young enough to practise all that is better in the new. He will be much missed by a host of grateful patients and by all his colleagues for his devotion to his calling. He was a devoted family man and leaves a widow and two children to whom we extend our sympathy.' By the time that's published my 'host of grateful patients' will be queueing up to see my successor and making odious comparisons."

"You're being pretty odious yourself," Sylvia said, "and you forgot about the 'long illness patiently borne'. Anyway it probably won't be like that at all. Knowing you, you'll outlive all of us and get one of those long tarra-diddles about being born in the year dot, driving a car up till the age of eighty-four, mental energy unabated, and dying in the home for Aged Doctors at the ripe old age of a hundred and three."

"You're thinking of the 'Home for Aged Horses'. No one's started one for doctors yet. It might be an idea though…"

"Tell me what he's like – Doctor Letchworth."

"You needn't change the subject, Sweetie. I was only joking. All doctors are like that. We are constantly imagining ourselves in the throes of some particularly nasty complaint from which there's little likelihood of recovery. It's an occupational hazard. Doesn't mean a thing. You must allow us our little neuroses."

"You mean like when you keep weighing yourself?"

"Sure. Faraday takes his own blood-pressure three times a day and a chap I knew in hospital used to keep his own temperature chart."

"And I had to marry one!" Sylvia said.

"Sorry?" I took her hands and pulled her to her feet.

"You know I am." The look in her eyes belied it.

"I don't know whether you've realised it," I said, "but we've been married for eight years."

"It seems like eight minutes."

"Any idea where the years have gone?"

"I haven't had time to notice."

"Neither have I. When we get Doctor Letchworth and Miss what's-her-name from Switzerland installed we shall have to slow up and take stock. If we don't before we know it we shall be in our dotage."

"I thought you were going to push off in the 'flower of your youth'?"

"Anyone can make a mistake."

"I'm pleased to hear it."

I put my arms round her. "Maybe it will be the Home for Aged Doctors after all."

"I shan't even mind that," Sylvia said, holding me tightly, "as long as they allow the Aged Wives to come as well."

Eleven

On 'the day' I got up early, wore a stiff collar, and shaved with particular care. In reply to Sylvia's enquiry as to whether I was going to a wedding I said no, but that my new assistant was starting work; one had to set an example.

Robin Letchworth beat me to it. As I went downstairs I saw a head silhouetted against the glass of the front door and he was waiting, complete with medical case, on the doorstep.

"Come in," I said, "and have some coffee with me while I try to put you in the picture a little. I expect we shall have an enormous crowd; we always do on Monday morning."

Robin watched me eat my toast while I tried to give him a general outline of the way in which I dealt with the patients and ran the practice.

"You aren't worried at all, are you?" I asked. And indeed he looked anything but. He was tall and good-looking, and he sat there woggling one leg which he had crossed over the other, as though he had not a care in the world.

I explained about the various ancillary services available in the district; what I did with my psychiatric problems; which of the 'notes for work' malingerers he should keep his eyes open for.

He looked at his watch. "Are we under starter's orders?"

"In five minutes we shall be off. I've no doubt they're standing round the walls."

We were to do the surgeries together. At the opposite end of the waiting-room to my own consulting room was a small room which had been used by my predecessor, and by ourselves until a week ago as a junk-room. We had now cleared out all the rubbish which had accumulated, as it invariably does in an unused room, and installed a desk, examination couch and chairs. The result of our efforts was that our loft, which had previously been full to overflowing, now *was* overflowing and that my assistant had an adequate, if not very large, consulting room in which to work. Caroline, whilst in bed, had written our two names artistically on pieces of card and I had drawing-pinned them to our respective doors. The patients had the choice; Doctor Letchworth or me.

"Shall we go?" I said.

Robin stood up. He looked like something out of *Tailor and Cutter* and I had wasted my efforts in setting a sartorial example.

"Ready when you are," he said.

We paused for a moment outside the waiting-room and I remembered my own hesitation and apprehension about facing for the first time the critical collection of patients waiting to see me when I was new to the practice. I gave Robin a reassuring smile. He grinned back confidently, seeming not in the slightest concerned. I remembered that he had had, of course, a good deal of experience in General Practice and was not beginning from scratch as I had done.

I superimposed my 'Good morning, all' expression on to my normal early-morning surliness and opened the waiting-room door, taking care not to swing it back on to anyone's toes.

The room was empty.

I looked at Robin. "It is Monday, isn't it?"

"As far as I know."

"Well, where is everybody?"

"Perhaps they heard I was coming," he volunteered.

"I can't understand it."

There was a scuffle which came from the door at the far side of the waiting-room which led into the street.

"*I* shall have something to say, any road," a voice I identified as belonging to Mrs Bridgewater, said. "*Me* with me veins!"

"Good lord," I said. "Sylvia must have forgotten to unlock the door!"

They were down the path and into the street standing there like disgruntled sheep among the prams, push-chairs and bicycles. My preliminary glance picked out Mrs Hawkins, Mr Grimes and Miss Tagg.

"Why didn't anyone ring the bell?" I said brightly as they filed past me.

"We did!"

"…kep' ringin' and ringin'…"

"Can't be workin'…"

I leaned round the lintel and pressed the bell-push. There was not a sound.

"Look, you start away," I said to Robin, "while I ask Sylvia to get somebody to see to the bell. It's going to be damned awkward without it."

"Sylvia!" I called up the stairs. "Sylvia!" There was no reply. I knocked on the banisters.

Penny's voice called, "Mummy's in the bathroom, and Peter's got a pain in his tummy again."

It was quicker to go up.

Sylvia fully dressed was sitting on the side of the bath.

"Do you know you forgot to unlock the waiting-room this morning?" I said. "You might be a bit more careful. They were queueing up down the…" And then Sylvia raised her head.

She was as yellow as the tiles surrounding the bath and her forehead was glistening.

"Sweetie, what is it?"

"I keep being sick," she whispered. "And I feel so faint."

"Oh God," I said. "Not you!"

I thought for a moment. It just had to happen then. Our daily help was away looking after her own children who had chicken-pox, my secretary was in hospital having a hysterectomy, the new help from Switzerland wasn't due until the evening. There were now four invalids and Sylvia was obviously in no state either to care for any of them or to answer the telephone. I made a quick decision. Caroline would have to curtail her convalescence and buckle-to.

I found her leaning over the wash-basin in her bedroom, greener than Sylvia.

"Doc," she said: "Cable home! Tell them I'm dying!"

At that moment the telephone rang.

I rushed into the bedroom and hurling myself across the unmade bed, picked up the receiver. "Hallo!"

"Darling, did you know it was Mink Week at Harrod's?"

"What number did you want?"

"6323. Where's Sophie?"

"I'm sorry. I haven't a clue!"

'Mink Week at Harrod's' indeed!

I replaced the receiver and the phone rang again immediately. I could hear Sylvia and Caroline groaning.

"Hallo."

"Doctor?"

"Yes."

"Mrs Carter, Doctor. Can you 'ave a look at my husband?"

"What's the matter with him?"

" 'E can't get out of bed." I imagined him bound and gagged but left it at that knowing I should get no further information without wasting a lot of time.

Penny came in in her nightie.

"Peter says his tummy ache's terree-bull!"

The phone rang.

"It's Mrs Pierce. I don't like to worry you, Doctor, knowing how busy you are but I think you should have a look at my mother-in-law."

"What's the matter with her?"

"She's on the floor."

"How do you mean?"

"Unconscious, Doctor."

"How long has she been like that?"

"Since about two o'clock this morning. Fred heard a noise and went down. She must have got up to get a drink of water."

"Why didn't you send for me?"

"I didn't like to disturb you. I know how busy you are…"

Penny came in.

"Peter says he thinks he's going to be sick and he wants Mummy. And Daddy, you know that itchy one on my foot…"

The phone rang.

I got Sylvia and Caroline to bed, both of them shivering and shaking and Caroline convinced that her last hour had come, and provided Peter with a bowl and Penny with instructions on what to do if he vomited.

Going down the stairs I thought, "Thank heavens for my assistant. At least I haven't fifty people to cope with as well."

But Robin was in the hall.

"What's the matter?" I said. "You can't have polished that lot off already?"

"Polished them off! I haven't seen a soul."

"Why on earth not?"

"I can't get them to come in to me. They all say they're waiting for you and every time I appear they look stolidly out of the window. I can hardly drag them by the scruffs of their necks."

"No," I said, feeling quite weak at the knees, "you certainly can't do that."

I sent Robin off to deal with Mrs Pierce's unconscious mother-in-law and in the waiting-room, now jammed solid, I made an announcement.

"Doctor Letchworth and I are both consulting," I said. "And anyone who would like to may be seen by my assistant. He'll be back here very soon and of course it will save a lot of waiting," I said with a winning smile. My audience looked unconvinced.

I went into my own consulting room and pressed the buzzer.

Two hours later Mr Thrupp came in, the last of thirty.

"I'm yer lot," he said, making himself comfortable on his chair. "Busy mornin'!"

But I was in no mood to exchange pleasantries. Mr Thrupp was holding a large, square basket on his lap.

I stamped the date viciously on to a prescription pad.

"What's the trouble?"

"Nothin's the trouble, as you might say."

I could see he meant to get his money's worth.

"What's the matter then?"

"There's nothin' the matter either."

I sat back and waited.

"I brought you sunthin'." He indicated the basket on his lap.

"For me?"

"Well for the kiddies really. You did mention as 'ow…" he opened the lid of the basket and a small puppy popped his head over the side and looked quiveringly at me with liquid eyes.

"The genuine harticle," Mr Thrupp said. "I was lucky to get it."

I was trying to think. An untrained puppy in addition to all my other domestic worries. Yet how could I refuse?

"…I knew 'is mother," Mr Thrupp was saying…"stood over two foot 'igh and a real lady."

"It's very kind of you, Mr Thrupp," I said: "you really shouldn't have troubled…"

" 'S'no trouble. We owe you something, me and the missus, so I said…"

"I supposed you couldn't…" I looked at his face suffused with his good deed. "…no, I don't suppose you could."

I let Mr Thrupp out of the waiting-room and with the puppy trembling under my arm knocked on Doctor Letchworth's door. There was no reply. The room was empty. I glanced at the day-book on the desk where he was to enter the name of every patient he saw. There was one entry: 'Miss Batchelor.' Miss Batchelor was aged eight years old and I presumed that she had come for some more of her mother's allergy tablets.

The house was quiet. In the kitchen breakfast dishes had been washed-up and put away.

Upstairs I said to Sylvia who was lying quite still and looking dreadful, "You shouldn't have gone downstairs, Sweetie. I told you to stay in bed."

"Downstairs?" she said. "My head is so painful I can't even turn over."

"Well, who washed-up the breakfast dishes?"

"I couldn't say," she groaned, and closed her eyes.

"How's the tummy now, Peter?" I said in the twins' bedroom.

"Oh it's fine."

"Rapid recovery," I commented. They were usually less willing to relinquish their symptoms so quickly.

"Doctor Letchworth made it better," Penny said. "What's that under your arm?"

"Doctor Letchworth? What was he doing up here?"

Penny said: "Peter thought he had appendicks so I went downstairs to call you and he was in the kitchen washing-up the breakfast."

"Who was?"

Penny sighed. "Doctor Letchworth." Then she shrieked. "Peter! Look, it's a puppy!" and startled by the noise the little fellow jumped from where he had been hiding under my arm, fell on to the carpet on his back, righted himself and scampered under the bed.

While Penny chased it I made sure that Peter's tummy ache had quite gone. As I tucked him in again Penny said:

"Daddy! Look what he's done on the carpet!" And I looked.

"You'd better mop it up before it stains."

Penny took her face-flannel from the wash-basin.

"No," I sighed. "Not with that."

I found the elusive Doctor Letchworth in Caroline's room. He was sitting on her bed, stroking her forehead and gazing into her eyes.

"There," he was saying softly. "There!"

"So there you are," I said heartily, feeling like a schoolmaster after a recalcitrant pupil. "Thanks for doing the dishes and looking after the invalids. I'm afraid you've started on rather an unfortunate day."

"Not at all," he said, smiling at Caroline. "I had to do something."

"Well, we'd better start on the visits," I said. "They can't refuse to see you if you turn up on the doorstep and we've over fifteen already."

He removed himself from Caroline's legs.

"Daddy!" a voice shrieked. "He's done it again!"

It was a day in a million and for that one could be glad. Caroline's temperature passed the hundred-and-one mark, Sylvia's the hundred-and-three. The phone didn't stop, the visits trickled in all day, Penny and Peter called out for an ingenious variety of trivia, and the puppy howled and wetted in the kitchen.

Robin made curried eggs for our lunch and the twins (who came choking down to the kitchen for glasses of water) and I washed-up. Sylvia and Caroline wanted nothing but to be left in peace although Caroline didn't seem adverse to Robin every now and then coming up to stroke her head.

Robin was a big help although not exactly in the capacity for which I had originally employed him.

"Jolly decent of you," I said when we had, between us, settled the invalids for the night and washed the supper dishes (omelets and chips – Robin had now completed his rather ovular repertoire).

"Not at all," he said. "I've enjoyed my first day. I've enjoyed it very much in fact. I'll come in early tomorrow and help you with breakfast."

I was embarrassed. "Don't bother," I said, "I shall be able to cope."

"No bother at all. I've nothing else to do." And he was gone.

There was a virus infection which was going round the district and it was this that Sylvia and Caroline seemed to have got. It was characterised by severe headache, vomiting and high temperature and lasted for about forty-eight hours.

"It's lousy, being ill," Sylvia said, sorry for herself as I came into the bedroom to prepare finally for bed.

"Poor Sweetie. I'm sorry there's nothing much I can do. By tomorrow night I promise you'll be feeling a great deal better."

Sylvia moved slightly and clutched her head. "I do hope you're right."

I had just taken off my trousers when there was a thumping of the front door-knocker and I remembered that I hadn't been on to the Electricity Company about the non-functioning bells. The knocking became more urgent as I struggled with my trousers which appeared suddenly and mysteriously to have only one leg. I buttoned them as I went down the stairs and wondered who had the infernal cheek to be ill at such an hour on such a day as the one I had survived.

At the door was Straker, the car-hire man, in his peaked, chauffeur's cap.

"I've brought her, Doctor. Sorry to be so late but the boat was five hours' late on account of the weather."

I must have looked blank.

"Your young lady from Switzerland." I peered into the darkness behind him and remembered the *au pair* we were expecting.

"She's in the car, Doctor. Shall I fetch her in?"

"Rather!" I said enthusiastically. "We could have done with her today."

Straker gave me a queer look and touching his cap turned back towards the car.

A few moments later I understood the significance of his glance.

Our new help had a smart fur coat, a hairstyle so *bouffant* you could hardly see her face, sensational legs and fourteen pieces of white luggage.

Straker was humming nonchalantly and looking at the ground.

I held out my hand to the apparition.

"Good evening," I said nervously, wondering what on earth Sylvia would say to this, "won't you come in?"

Twelve

She stood in the hall in an aura of expensive perfume and looked at me expectantly.

"Listen," I said, "stand there a moment and don't move." And as an afterthought, "I say, you do speak English, don't you?"

"Leetle."

"Fine. I shan't be a moment."

Upstairs I said to Sylvia: "Sweetie, it's the *au pair*. Straker's just delivered her."

"Mmm." She was under the covers.

"Darling, what shall I do with her?"

"Ugh." This time it was a groan.

"Sweetie!" I pleaded.

"Give her a cup of tea or something and put her to bed," came the muffled decree from beneath the blankets.

At least it was a lead.

When I was at the door Sylvia said: "What's she like?"

I swallowed, thinking of the legs and the luggage. "Oh fine," I lied. "I'm sure she'll be a great deal of help."

She was re-doing her lips in front of the hall mirror.

"Well," I said brightly. "What about something to drink?"

The effect was immediate. She put away the lipstick, shrugged off the coat beneath which was a tight-fitting pale blue suit and said:

120

" 'Ow nice!"

"Good." We were getting somewhere. "What would you like?"

"Visky?" she suggested. "Geen?"

It was, I suppose, my fault for not making myself clear. I should have said tea or coffee. Now it was too late. I led her into the morning-room and dispensed a not very large whisky.

Her nails were about an inch long and as pointed as a tiger's. I wondered what they would be like after a week of washing-up.

Weary as I was I remembered my manners. I asked how had the journey been; " 'orrible." What was the weather like in Switzerland; " 'orrible." I changed my tactics. Had she ever done any domestic work before?

"Domesteek?"

"Yes. That's right. You know, washing-up and all that."

She laughed a silvery laugh.

"Plees," she said, on a new tack, the last topic, I gathered, not being too popular. "I would like to up-ring my friend."

"Of course," I said, indicating the telephone, "although it's a bit late."

She shook her head and tutted in disagreement while dialling the number which she followed from a piece of paper which she had taken from her crocodile handbag.

"She don't never in bed before three-four o'clock," and I wondered what sort of peculiar people her friend could be working for when I heard her say:

"Claridge 'otel? Please, Count Menotti." And then to me: "She comes."

"She?"

"My boyfriend."

"You mean 'he'," I said. But she was standing up and blowing impassioned kisses into the receiver.

"Riffi!" she shouted. "Riffi, darling." And then she kicked off her shoes with emotion and relapsed into a stream of what I presumed was Swiss–German which at first was interspersed

121

with countless, 'nein, nein, nein's and later developed into a cacophony of 'ja, ja, ja's. When the 'ja's had reached what appeared to be their climax she held one hand over the mouthpiece and whispered to me, "Plees, have I free tomorrow?"

"Tomorrow?" I said. "You've only just arrived. Besides my wife is ill."

Her face fell and she resorted back to Riffi and the 'nein, nein, nein' routine.

I gave her two more minutes then said: "Look here, I'm afraid we can't keep the telephone for so long in this house. Patients might be trying to get through." She nodded at me although I don't think she understood because the conversation, which seemed to be rather one-sided, went on. Then, with what seemed to be extraordinary suddenness she blew two more kisses, slipped her feet into her shoes and replaced the receiver with a bang.

She sighed.

"My friend!" she said. I suppose she felt she owed me an explanation.

I stood up purposefully and looked at my watch.

"Now," I said firmly, "I'll show you your room and you'd better go to bed."

"Ja."

A doubt assailed me. "Are you hungry or anything?"

"Hungrig?"

"Yes."

She clasped her stomach, rolled her eyes and made an up and down motion with her hand. "So, ze boat. I will nussing."

"OK," I said relieved. "Let's go."

She stood looking with disgust round her bedroom while I carried fourteen pieces of white luggage up the stairs. I agreed it wasn't very large, but it was pretty, comfortable and bright and even had a radio.

She peered into the small wardrobe, then looked round helplessly and indicated the luggage piled high on the bed, the chair and the floor.

"My sings?" she said. "Is no place!"

But I'd had enough.

"My wife will sort you out in the morning," I said. "Now you must go to bed. I'm tired if you're not."

"You 'ave a wife?" she said, staring at me.

"I told you before. She's ill."

"Peety!" I wasn't sure if she was mourning the fact that I had a wife or that she was ill but I didn't pursue the matter.

I wished her good night and shut the door.

In the bedroom, Sylvia was asleep. I had just removed my trousers for the second time when there was a knock at the door.

I put my head round it.

"Plees," Miss Winterhalter said, "toilet?"

I hadn't been a very good host. But after I'd pointed out that the room she required was next to her own and that the door had been wide open it occurred to me that she was not so much lost as eager to show me the pink nylon negligee in which I had to admit she looked extremely fetching.

In the morning Sylvia seemed a little better and volunteered to get up. She was really in no state to though, and I'm sure she was relieved when I insisted that she stay in bed.

"How will you manage?" she said. "You can't let Doctor Letchworth do the dishes again."

"You forget we have Miss Winterhalter."

"Of course. I was forgetting her."

"I'll go and wake her. Hasn't she another name? I can't keep calling her Miss Winterhalter."

"Charlotta," Sylvia said and went back to sleep.

I knocked gently on her door. "Charlotta!" Nothing. "Charlotta!"

I knocked more loudly. Called more loudly. Waited, then went in.

The covers were only up to her waist, her nightdress was diaphanous and she appeared still to be sleeping. Again I called her name; again there was no response; so I took her by the shoulder and shook her.

"Riffi!" she shouted ecstatically and flung her arms round my neck, pulling me down towards her.

"Charlotta!" I said severely, disentangling myself. "It's time to get up!"

She immediately released me, orientated herself and looked with incredulity at the tiny clock by her bedside.

"Now?"

"Yes."

"So early?"

"Yes. Hurry up, please. The children have to have breakfast."

"May I take a bath?"

"If you aren't too long."

She flung back the bedclothes so I left.

An hour later, when Robin and I between us had given breakfast to Sylvia, Caroline and the twins who were all on the mend, Miss Winterhalter appeared. She knocked on the door of my surgery while I was examining Mr Harper.

"Please," she said, and a waiting-room of curious people hung on her words, "I'm ready."

I left Mr Harper to dress and showed her the way to the kitchen. It was littered with the remains of breakfast and the puppy had been bestowing his attentions on the floor. I had to admit that it didn't look very appetising. Miss Winterhalter appeared about to be sick.

I dealt with the puppy's contribution. "Just a baby," I said heartily in mitigation, poiting to the little fellow who sat in the cardboard box we had given him, his head on one side appealingly. "A patient of mine gave it to us for the children. We'll soon have him house-trained."

Miss Winterhalter, in light skirt and pale pink sweater, appeared unmoved. I gave her an apron of Sylvia's, told her to take some breakfast for herself and left her to it.

In the waiting-room the heavy odour of Lanvin's Arpège lingered in the air. Mr Harper, now dressed, was curious.

" 'oo was that, Doc?"

"Our new maid."

He gave me a big wink.

There were eighteen people after Mr Harper. They all enquired who she was. The reaction of the men was much the same as that of Mr Harper; that of the women far more practical. To a woman they were of the opinion that Charlotta would be useless. They had had some, they said, and they knew. The only person who had any useful contribution to make was Mrs Hampton who said that she wished she had known we needed somebody as her Italian maid had a friend who was coming over from Genoa and would need a job.

When they'd all gone, I opened the windows wide in the waiting-room to disperse the heavy smell of perfume, now mingled with less pleasant odours, and went to see how Charlotta was getting on.

She was sitting on a chair in the kitchen, smoking a cigarette in a long green holder and drinking coffee. The breakfast dishes were still in the same place. Of the puppy there was no sign.

"Where's the dog?" I demanded.

She pointed to the back door.

The garden was empty, and the side gate wide open.

"He's only a baby," I said, "you mustn't put him out by himself!"

She smiled in agreement, blew a smoke ring and topped up her coffee-cup.

The front doorbell rang. Opening it I could see no one. Then I looked down. Penny, barefoot and in her pyjamas was holding the puppy.

"Penny, where have you been?"

"I was looking out of the window and I saw him go down the road. The door must've shut."

I was glad to get out and do the visits.

When I got back Sylvia and Caroline were creeping round a tidy kitchen like a couple of zombies, in their dressing-gowns, preparing lunch.

"Where's Miss Winterhalter?"

"Gone," Sylvia said.

"Gone?"

"A Caddy a block and a half long came for her."

"She's taken her luggage?"

"Fourteen pieces."

"Well," I said inadequately, "that's that." And then, at the same time as I remembered what Mrs Hampton had said about having a maid to spare, I felt a pain like a knife in my abdomen.

"Ouch!" I said.

Sylvia said: "What is it, Sweetie?"

But I was on my way to the bathroom.

I am convinced that every Medical Practitioner should be ill occasionally. It was a strange thing suddenly to be looking at medicine from the subjective side but I'm sure that it benefited my practice of the healing art. All at once I had a taste of how the patient, beneath the sheets, felt. In twenty-four unpleasant hours I discovered why they moaned, groaned and clutched their heads; why they were often disinclined to talk; why, in short, they felt sorry for themselves and frequently believed their last hours had arrived. I experienced, instead of hearing about, the aching limbs, the fleeting pains, the painful eye movements, the nausea. When Robin Letchworth came in cheerily to see me, I saw myself, bright with *bonhomie*, entering the sick-room of a patient, and the boot, with a vengeance, was all at once upon the other foot.

He laughed and said: "You'll be all right, old chap," when what I wanted was sympathy; I was quite well aware that I would be 'all right'. He sat on the bed and bounced, when the slightest movement sent fantastic pains shooting through my head. He chatted to Sylvia and Caroline who had congregated in my sick-room about anything and everything as though I didn't exist, when what I wanted was a little attention. Finally, he went out and slammed the door.

Of course it was wonderful having him. Previously one of my worst worries had been what would happen to my practice should I become ill. It was an anxiety common amongst single-handed practitioners. It wasn't really the short-term illnesses we worried about either. It was the more serious ones. A locum for more than a week or so at a time was enough to leave any of us looking gravely at our bank statements. Now, thanks to Robin, I didn't have to worry about the practice. My indisposition was even, in a way, a good thing. The patients had no choice, if they wished to be seen, but to consult my assistant. They would have to get to know him whether they liked him or not.

I was not short of nurses. Sylvia and Caroline, neither of them really fit, were wonderful. They said I was a ghastly patient to look after but look after me they did. I suppose I did drive them a bit mad. Each time the bell rang I wanted to know who was at the door. At each telephone call I insisted on knowing who had rung. Finally they gave me an ultimatum.

"Either you shut up and be properly ill," Sylvia said darkly, "or we shall leave you to rot. Doctor Letchworth is coping beautifully with everything and you haven't a thing to worry about. And what's more, you can stop taking your temperature every ten minutes. You'll wear the thermometer out."

"I may be cooking up a cerebro-spinal meningitis," I said importantly. "I have an extremely bad headache and I think my back's getting a bit stiff."

"Rubbish!" Sylvia said. "You've exactly the same as Caroline and I had, you're getting a lot more attention than we had and you'll be much better in the morning."

And I had to be satisfied with that.

I wasn't short of messengers. Penny and Peter were most solicitous and ran up and down umpteen times with newspapers, letters, books I didn't read, and glasses of water the contents of which were usually liberally sloshed on to the stairs on the way up. They also kept me informed about the doings of the puppy, whose misdeeds they described in the greatest detail, and came up for adjudication to my sick-room on my second day in bed, over his name about which they were squabbling.

"I think 'Miss Woodcock'," Penny said.

Peter said, "That's silly!"

And I said, "You can't call it after your teacher. It isn't very polite. Besides which you don't call dogs 'Miss'."

"Why not?"

"You just don't."

"I don't see why not!"

"Isobel?" Peter suggested. Isobel was his girlfriend from down the road.

"Not after friends either. It has to be a doggy name. Besides which it happens to be a boy dog."

"How do you know?"

"Mr Harper told me."

"How does he know?"

"I'll explain when I'm better."

"When will you be better?"

"In a day or two."

"You aren't going to die then?" Peter said.

"No." I was curious. "Why?"

"Mummy told Aunt Caroline you thought you were dying."

"It was only a joke," I reassured him. He looked disappointed.

"What's the matter?"

"I wanted your stethoscope."

"About the dog," I said.

"Noddy!"

"Big-Ears!"

"You must be more original."

"Original!"

I sighed. "What about Blackie? He is, after all, black."

They looked at me pityingly.

"Let's ask Mummy," I said brightly, passing the buck to Sylvia who had just come in with tea.

"As far as I'm concerned he's a liability," Sylvia said.

And 'Liability' he remained, with 'Billy' conveniently for short.

Sylvia had brought the tea-tray and Caroline the teapot. They sat on the bed to keep me company. Caroline had taken to wearing a head-scarf tied gypsy-wise and I had become so used to seeing it that it was difficult almost to remember how she had looked before.

The telephone rang and we all jumped, sending biscuits over the eiderdown.

I got there first. It was Faraday.

"I'm surprised to hear your voice," he said.

"Why's that?"

"I heard you were desperately ill. That's why I'm phoning."

"Who told you?"

"Mrs Dangerfield. Your assistant sent her to my Out-patients."

"I've caught a bug from my patients."

Faraday laughed raucously.

"What's so funny?" I said touchily.

"The 'biter bit' and all that."

"Glad you're amused."

"I really phoned to remind you about the dance."

"The dance?"

"A week on Saturday."

"Of course, the Medical Dance."

"I doubt if I shall be fit enough."

"You'd better be. I'm relying on you. Take some of your own medicine."

"How frightfully funny!"

"I'll call round at eight. We'll have drinks at your place. Must go, I'm in the middle of a lumbar puncture."

"Thanks for phoning," I said, but he'd gone.

"That was Faraday," I said to Sylvia and Caroline who had eaten all my biscuits while I had been talking, "to remind us about the dance on Saturday week. I presume you girls are coming. It will probably be quite jolly."

"All right," Sylvia said. "It's ages since we've been out."

I looked at Caroline, always ready for fun.

"You can count me out," she said.

"Why?"

"I have a date."

"Who with?"

"I have to wash my smalls."

And then I remembered her hair. Sylvia was glaring at me and I could see how tactless I had been.

"Well, never mind," I said feebly. "I expect we shall be glad of a sitter."

Thirteen

Robin Letchworth was an enormous success. My few days off sick had come at the right moment and the patients in the waiting-room were no longer afraid of the unknown ogre behind the unfamiliar door.

On my first day back in harness things went unbelievably smoothly. There was no more staring obtusely out of the window when Robin opened his door, no more mumbled apologies for preferring to consult me. Patients came to whichever one of us was free first and seemed grateful for not having to wait so long in the waiting-room, which was of course the general idea.

It was hard to believe how accustomed I had become to rushing my work in a manner which was beneficial neither to the patients nor to myself. Now, for the first time in years, I had leisure to hear the history at the pace at which the patient wished to tell it, and listen to the full story without the feeling of irritation brought on by the knowledge that behind the door was a packed waiting-room which it seemed impossible to clear in reasonable time.

This was medicine and I enjoyed practising it.

Not all the patients took it the same way.

Old Mr Lambert, struggling with his shaking, nobbly fingers to fasten the buttons of his waistcoat, said: "I hope it's not a liberty, Doctor, but there's something I'd like to ask you."

"Ask away." I leaned back in my swivel chair.

Mr Lambert came close to the desk and leaned towards me.

"Is there anything the matter with me?"

"Nothing more than usual," I said, surprised. By usual I meant the arthritis from which he had suffered for over thirty years. "As a matter of fact you seem to be in very good shape. Eighty-eight, isn't it?" I said, looking for his notes with the date of birth.

"Eighty-nine, Midsummer Day."

"No one would believe it. Why do you ask?"

"Well, Doctor, it's like this." He shrugged into his jacket and sat down leaning forwards on his stick. "I bin in here half an hour!"

"Yes?"

"Well, begging your pardon, Doctor, I was getting worried. It's more often than not: 'Good morning, Mr Lambert, how are you? Struggling along? That's good! Here's your medicine; come back in a week's time. Goodbye.' "

It was a pretty fair imitation of myself. My old self.

"So you see, Doctor, when you told me to take me clothes off and lay down, I was worried. There's nothing wrong, is there?"

"Nothing at all."

"You'd tell me, wouldn't you? They just took my neighbour off with the kidneys."

I reassured the old man to the best of my ability, but he left looking less happy than on any of his weekly visits during the past eight years.

Mr Lambert had brought some home truths to light: Mrs Sage hammered them home. It was when I visited her little girl. Patricia had tonsilitis and earache. I examined and prescribed for her and was on my way downstairs when Mrs Sage said: "I know it's no use offering you a cup of tea, Doctor," and held open the front door.

I didn't go out. I said: "Why not?"

Mrs Sage looked embarrassed. "Well, we all gave up doing that years ago. When you stopped taking your coat off."

It was my turn to be embarrassed. "All?"

"Everyone in the road. *Most* of us *understand*, of course, how busy you are these days."

"And the others?"

"Well, you know how it is Doctor. Some people haven't got used to this Health Service business and think it should be more like the old days."

"You mean people like Mrs Walker and the Southcott's?" Two families who had gone off my list.

"They didn't like you running up the path. It made them nervous."

"Is that what I do?" I hadn't been aware of it.

"Run up the path; stairs two at a time; directions about the medicine while you're running out again. Sometimes I'd think it was my imagination that you'd called at all if it wasn't for the prescription in my hand."

I looked at her.

"That's very interesting," I said. "I shan't be running any more. I have an assistant now to help me."

"I'm so glad, Doctor. I'm sure it wasn't good for you, rushing around like that."

"If you really meant it about the cup of tea?"

"Of course. I'm going to have one."

"Then I'll join you."

"I'm terribly pleased. No one will believe it." She shut the door again and held out her hand.

"Won't you take your coat off?"

By the end of the week things had improved on all fronts. The practice was running smoothly, all the invalids were mobile and we also, by courtesy of Mrs Hampton whose maid's friend she was, had Maria. Maria was everything that Miss Winter-halter had not been. She was a plain-looking little thing who darted about as efficiently as a bird, she thought her room delightful and, most wonderful of all, she adored children and dogs. 'Beely', as she called him, brought out all the maternal instincts powerful, so I was told, in the Italian breast. Together with the twins, Beely and Maria formed an alliance of four unshakable in their loyalty to each other. When Beely misbehaved he was excused on grounds of his extreme youth; when the twins shot a rocket from the cornflakes box through the surgery window they were clasped to Maria's bosom from which touching tableau she pleaded on their behalf for mercy, tears in her wide brown eyes; when Maria dropped the gravy-boat it was the twins who immediately opened their money-box. If it was a syndicate that lent itself to abuse it did at least bring peace. We were happy to turn a fair number of blind eyes and let the four of them get on with it. Of Maria's work Sylvia had no cause to complain, and the household chugged slowly back to normal.

Only Caroline, still, poor thing, in her headscarf, hadn't the courage to leave the house.

"You look fine," I tried to encourage her, "doesn't she, Robin?"

"Delectable!" Robin said, checking his visiting list.

"Honestly, Caroline, people go out in head-scarves when they've masses of hair underneath. You've done it yourself."

"I've nothing to go out for," she said. "I've kinda lost interest in Sex." But I knew that what she'd lost was confidence in herself and that it was up to Sylvia and me to help her.

I discussed the problem with Sylvia but to my surprise she just looked mysterious and made some enigmatic and unhelpful remarks to the effect that Caroline would be 'all right'.

It was the Saturday night of the Medical Dance before I discovered what it was all about.

Sylvia and Caroline spent the whole of Saturday closeted in Caroline's bedroom. From the landing I heard an extraordinary mixture of whisperings, rumblings, groans, moans and sudden hysterical shrieks of wild laughter. They appeared for lunch and afterwards went straight back. At five o'clock I knocked upon the locked door and told Sylvia to be sure to get changed in time as Faraday would be arriving at eight. I also suggested that she might like to get my things ready for me. The suggestion was received with what sounded like a grunt so I gave up and went down to the surgery.

We had a fair number for a Saturday night when we usually had to compete with the pubs and the cinema.

When I pressed the buzzer for the last patient it was Faraday who came in from the waiting-room, in evening dress.

"What on earth are you doing in there?" I said.

He sat down and took off his shoes.

"It's me feet, Doctor."

"What's the matter with them?"

He wriggled his toes. "My shoes are too tight. I had to borrow them from the RMO. I suppose you haven't any spare black?"

"It depends what size."

"Thirteen and a half."

"You should ask an elephant. What were you doing in the waiting-room?"

He indicated his dinner-jacket.

"I thought you might like a bit of tone added to the place."

"You know for a Consultant you really ought to grow up a bit. People won't have any confidence in you. They like their Consultant to be a kind of Father figure."

He was nosing round my drugs cupboard, not listening. He picked up an ampoule and threw it into the trash bin.

"What was that?"

"Folic Acid. No one uses that any more. Get better results with B.12."

"Thanks," I said.

"Not at all." He slapped me on the back. "Come on, Sobersides, lead me to the drinks."

"What about your shoes?" I said at the door. "The RMO's," he said and went back to collect them.

135

In the lounge, Sylvia, superb in white satin, was mixing Martinis.

"You've done it on purpose to disturb my equilibrium," Faraday said, kissing her.

"You mean the Martinis?" she said.

"No, you."

"I've something else for your equilibrium," she said and looked towards the door. We followed her glance and there in the doorway was Caroline, or at least I presumed it was, and I discovered what the secret conference had been about all day.

She was wearing a black velvet dress, very tight fitting indeed until it reached the lower hip region from where it flowed into an elegant sort of fish-tail. The bodice was cut not too high to arouse your interest but high enough to keep you guessing. Above it her shoulders were like honey-coloured silk. She wore a deep peach lipstick, blue stuff on her eyelids and sparkling earrings. Most surprising of all, she had a mass of strawberry blonde hair swirled into an exotic doughnut on top of her head. She looked more than sensational.

I looked behind to see the effect she was having on Faraday but he was struggling to get his feet into the RMO's shoes.

"Caroline," I said. "Words fail me!" And it was more than her appearance. With the dress and the wig, which I presumed was Sylvia's doing, she had regained her old sunny smile and composure. I realised just how miserable she must have been.

At the Society of General Medicine we were received by Sir Neville and Lady Carter-Browne to whom our names were announced by a red-coated toastmaster with a voice like a powerful foghorn and a cauliflower ear. Sir Neville was the President of the Society and the strain of being the President's wife had apparently reduced the handshake of his good lady to that of a wet fish. According to Faraday, who must have gazed more deeply into her eyes than I, she also seemed to have a slight nystagmus and I'm sure that all evening he was worrying, in addition to the discomfort of his feet, about its cause.

The reception-room was packed. In the company of doctors' wives, not renowned for their looks or sartorial splendour, Sylvia and Caroline were outstanding. Many groups through which we elbowed our way on our journey to the bar stopped in mid-delivery or anaesthetics sessions to goggle at them. When they resumed their conversations I'm sure that many of them had forgotten what it was they had been talking about.

At dinner we had been placed at a table with the Pathologist from Faraday's hospital, whose wife worked in the Diatetic Department, a Surgeon who was renowned as much for his taciturnity as for his skill with the knife, the former being due, it was said, to his wife who suffered from a complaint known in medical circles as 'verbal diarrhoea', and a GP from Luton whose wife looked as though she could pick him up in one hand and put him in her pocket. It was next to this mountain of good-natured flesh that Faraday elected to sit.

Before dinner was announced he had hustled me furtively into the ballroom and at table sixteen had deftly and expertly altered the place-cards from their original positions.

I was surprised. "Wouldn't you rather sit next to Mrs Medway?" I said. She was the Pathologist's wife and a nice girl.

"No future in it. I've got to charm the GPs."

And then I remembered, Faraday was in need of patients.

We were halfway through the grapefruit, and Mrs Scott, the Surgeon's wife, was saying: "There's one thing about these medical dinners, as I always say to my husband, isn't that true, dear, Mr Scott usually agrees with me, you can always rely on…"

But we never, fortunately, discovered what it was that you could always rely on for at the moment the toastmaster made an announcement through the loudspeaker on the dais: "Dr Faraday is wanted on the telephone please. Dr Faraday."

This announcement was greeted with a burst of applause from the assembled company of merry, relaxed, medical men, who presumed, as one always did on these occasions, that it was a call to work for somebody else.

After five minutes Faraday was back.

"A visit?" the GP's wife said sympathetically as he took his seat again next to her.

"No," Faraday said.

"You are in General Practice, aren't you?"

"As a matter of fact, no," Faraday said, trying to polish off his grapefruit at the same time. "I'm a *Neurologist*." This last as loudly as he dared.

The stout lady thought for a moment. "The name rings a bell," she said thoughtfully and turned to her husband. "Dr Faraday's a Neurologist, Arthur," she said. And to Faraday: "My husband has a practice in Luton."

"Oh really?" Faraday said innocently as though he hadn't already gone to considerable lengths to find out. "A delightful part of the country."

I almost choked over my soup but had to admire his tactics. Contact had been established. Faraday was now talking to the little GP from Luton across his wife's bosom.

The toastmaster was kept busy. There was a call for Doctor Avery and one for Doctor Pink who didn't return for the rest of the evening. With the roast duck there was another for Faraday.

When he got back Sylvia said: "You're very popular tonight."

Faraday shrugged modestly. "GPs," he said, "keep ringing me up for consultations."

Mrs Scott, wife of the silent surgeon, was saying: "I know it's no business of mine but I do think that they ought to make these sessions begin..." when I noticed that her husband, although dissecting his duck with as much concentration as if he were doing a partial gastrectomy, had his thigh tightly pressed against Caroline's.

We had waded our way through the Ice Pudding, the Petit Fours and the equivalent of at least three LP's of Mrs Scott's vapid opinions which dripped from her tongue like water from a washerless tap, and had settled down to the cigars, the coffee and the speeches, when Faraday, for the third time, was called to the telephone.

He crept back, quiet as a mouse, while Sir Neville Carter-Browne, not renowned as an after-dinner speaker, was in mid anecdote. I tried to catch his eye, but got the distinct impression that Faraday deliberately looked the other way. I'm sure he could not have been that anxious to get to his exceedingly poor brandy.

Doctors are not good dancers. Perhaps they don't get enough practice, and their wives are too busy being good little ancillaries to do anything about it. Anyway the bands on these occasions always avoided showing us up too much by sticking to the good, old-fashioned rhythms and keeping the Mambo-Wambo's or whatever the current fashion was for the more practised assemblies of Boilermakers' Unions or teenage Charity Dances.

We all had an amble round the floor, usually interrupted by a discussion with someone we bumped into about a mutual patient or the ubiquitous Health Service. Caroline was never off it.

Mr Scott, her silent dinner-partner, tried to monopolise her. Each time he danced with her his hand crept farther and farther down her back. His wife, who had button-holed the poor Pathologist and was treating him to an exposition of her views of Hospital Management, either did not notice or did not care. A paediatrician, a radiologist and a Canadian nuclear physicist, also queued up for Caroline's favours. When she bestowed them upon anyone but himself Mr Scott drank whisky and glowered, his eyes never leaving the front of her dress for a moment.

Faraday hadn't danced at all. Towards the end of the evening while Mr Scott was doing a duty dance with his wife who had insisted, and Sylvia was gossiping in the powder-room, he, Caroline and I were alone at the table. Caroline was staring at

Faraday with a funny sort of look in her eyes. Faraday was making notes on the back of a menu.

"Why don't you dance with the lady," I said, reminding him of his duty.

He said nothing but swung his long legs up from beneath the table. He was sitting in his socks.

"He's having trouble with his feet," I said, defending him, to Caroline.

"There's nothing the matter with my feet," Faraday said indignantly. "You'd not find a healthier pair in the whole room. It's the RMO's shoes!" And just then he was called, for the fourth time, to the telephone.

When he got back, having walked nonchalantly to the foyer and back in his nylon socks, I said:

"Don't tell me another GP wants a consultation!"

"Good lord, no!" he said. "It was the RMO."

"I suppose he wants his shoes back?" Faraday was struggling to get his feet into them.

"No. They're mine till tomorrow. By which time I shall probably need the attentions of an orthopaedic surgeon." He stood up.

"Where are you going?"

"I'm pushing off. To the Consultation!"

"But I thought you said it was the RMO."

He sighed. "It was, you clot. There must be a hundred GPs here. At least half of them will now remember my name."

"You mean you *fixed* all those calls?"

Faraday grinned. "Every hour on the hour. If anyone wants to know where I am tell them it's an acute 'trigeminal neuralgia' – at the Bunch of Grapes in Fulham!"

"You can't say he doesn't try!" I said to Caroline as I watched Faraday weave his way through the ballroom, slapping the odd acquaintance jovially on the back as he went.

Caroline was staring at his broad, athletic back, topped by the uncurbable tufts of fair hair.

"Doc," she breathed, not taking her eyes off Faraday. "Did you hear the click?"

"What click?"

"The penny's dropped!"

I tried to think.

"Man the lifeboats!" my unpredictable cousin said, still staring at the doors through which Faraday had now disappeared; "I've got the mating urge!"

Fourteen

Caroline normally, with her odd Transatlantic ideas, her fads and her fancies, was a disturbing influence in the house; Caroline in love was almost more than we could stand.

She moaned, moped, drifted round muttering to herself, stopped eating – even yoghurt – sang sentimental songs in a cracked voice, didn't answer when she was spoken to, and read poetry aloud.

It seemed to be a one-sided affair. When I spoke to Faraday on the phone, I said:

"Did you enjoy the dance?"

"Except for my feet. They'll never be the same again."

"Damn your feet. I'm fed up with hearing about them. Caroline's a nice girl, isn't she?"

"Charming. How's Sylvia?"

"Fine. What did you think of her dress?"

"Terrific. I adore her in white."

"I mean Caroline's!"

"I can't say I care for pink."

"It was black!"

"Of course. Stupid of me."

It was obvious I was flogging a dead horse.

When Caroline began to lose the bounce from her curves and her cheek looked sunken it became obvious that something would have to be done. We couldn't let her fade away from unrequited love.

Sylvia, always full of bright ideas, suggested that we invite Faraday for the weekend so that Caroline had at least a chance to wriggle her way into his affections.

"It's a good plan," I said, "but there's a snag."

"What's that?"

"Caroline's occupying the spare bedroom."

"Perhaps that would be the answer to the whole problem," Sylvia said brightly.

"Maybe. But I don't intend to be responsible. Caroline is my cousin, remember."

"There are times when I wonder if you remember."

I ignored the insinuation.

"Anyway," Sylvia said, "it's perfectly simple. Faraday can have the camp-bed in with the children."

"I should think it would be better," I said, "if Caroline went in with the children and we put Faraday in Caroline's room."

As usual I should have listened to my helpmeet.

Faraday, only too willing to accept our invitation on his first free weekend, arrived one Friday night a month later and installed himself comfortably in Caroline's bedroom. Caroline, although having appeared to move most of her belongings next door into the children's room, discovered that the articles of which she was in most dire need, she had left behind. In particular when Faraday was in his bedroom.

She tried every trick in the book and even I had to admit that in Caroline's book there was no shortage of tricks. She wandered into his room in her nightie, innocently unaware that he was there; she read up some of my Neurology books and tried to impress him with her knowledge of his subject; she even mended his socks, and Caroline hadn't mended a thing since she had been with us. At meal-times it was positively embarrassing. She just sat opposite him, leaned her chin on her hands, and stared. Faraday, apparently quite oblivious, ate heartily, chattered endlessly, and complimented Sylvia on her cooking. On Saturday Caroline changed her place over and sat beside him from where her hand could brush his at opportune moments or her cheek touch his knee as she bent to retrieve her napkin. The results were the same: nil.

By Saturday night Caroline was becoming desperate. At seven-thirty she waylaid me on my way out of the surgery and said that she had a plan. "Good for you!" I said, still thinking of Mr Sowerby's abdominal pain for which I was unable to find a reason. Then she told me the plan.

It was quite a simple one. Sylvia was out for the evening visiting her girl-friend who had just had a baby. That left Caroline as the entrepreneur, me as the decoy and Faraday as the sitting duck. The idea was this: Faraday had told us he had some notes to write up in his room after supper. Caroline and I were to be clinched in a passionate embrace in the sitting-room, the door of which would be wide open, at the precise moment when one of the twins, previously primed, would knock on Faraday's door and beg piteously for a drink of water. Poor, soft-hearted Faraday, moved by the plea, was to come down to the kitchen, passing the sitting-room on his way and become madly inflamed with jealousy at what he saw…

"I'm sorry, dear," I said to Caroline. "Much as I sympathise with your condition, I am not prepared to co-operate to quite such an extent."

"Am I so repulsive?"

"It isn't that. I'm a married man."

"It could be a cousinly kiss."

"I doubt if that would inflame anyone with jealousy."

"You don't have to put your heart in it. No one would ever know. It will be all over by the time Sylvia comes back."

"I'm sorry. You'll have to think of something else."

But after supper Caroline was in such a state that I relented.

By nine o'clock, Faraday had gone up to his room, Penny had rehearsed her part and everything appeared to be going according to plan.

In the sitting-room we set the stage. We pulled the sofa round so that it was facing the door, scattered it with cushions, we didn't after all want to be uncomfortable, and synchronised our watches. Zero hour was nine-thirty. Penny, thrilled with the importance of the task she had been given, was to go in to Faraday at nine twenty-eight. Peter who had just learned to tell the time, had the subsidiary task of giving her her cue. Caroline had bribed them to stay awake with candy bars.

I began to feel nervous. Caroline kicked off her shoes.

"Hey!" I said. "What's that for?"

"You can't make passionate love with your shoes on."

"Who said anything about passionate love? I agreed to one kiss."

"Technicality," she said briskly: "It's a pity I can't disarrange my hair." She now had half an inch of hair which had grown in tight curls all over her head. The boyish style suited her and she no longer worried about her appearance.

She took the belt off her dress and pulled my tie round until the knot was beneath my ear.

"There!" she said. "That will do for a start." She sat down and patted the sofa next to her. "C'mon," she coaxed. "It's only little Cousin Caroline. Remember?"

"That's just the trouble." I sat on the edge of the sofa about two feet away from her.

Caroline sighed. "This is not going to be easy."

She looked at her watch. "It's almost twenty after. We shall have to hurry."

But I felt no more like getting into a clinch with Caroline than jumping into a cold bath.

"I can see," she said, "that I shall have to seduce you."

I moved away until I was huddled up against the arm of the sofa.

"Don't be scared," Caroline said. "This is what happens to uneducated teenagers in the backs of cars and accounts for fifty-nine point nine per cent of babies born to unmarried mothers in the State of…"

"I object…"

"What to?"

"I am not an uneducated teenager. Neither, incidentally, is this the back of a car."

Caroline put her hand over my mouth. "Now ssh!" she said. "You've wasted three and a half minutes." She lowered her hand and with it covered my own. Her fingers were cool.

"The first contact between the boy and girl is normally that of the hands. This touch sets, as it were, the motor in motion, the wheels turning, though at the moment, not too fast…"

I found her touch not unpleasant although I couldn't exactly say that my wheels had begun to turn.

"…with the intertwining of the fingers, more sensitive skin areas are approached with the result that the pulse beats quicken and a pleasurable sensation, associated with warm and a kinda tingling engulfs the participants…"

Caroline glanced at her watch and I'm certain that in view of the limited time at our disposal cut out a few of the logical states, for almost before I knew it she had her arms round me and was stroking a particularly sensitive spot I have at the back of my neck. I couldn't, by any stretching of the imagination, have called it unpleasant. Deciding that I had better make the best of it, I decided to relax and pulling Caroline with me lay back upon the cushions. I must have overdone the relaxing, however, and dozed off because the next thing I remember was opening my eyes and noticing that the time on Caroline's watch which was about an inch away from my eye, was twenty to ten.

I tried to get up but about nine and a half stone of pure woman prevented me.

"Cousin Caroline," I said severely, "something, somewhere, appears to have gone wrong."

She heaved herself off me and looked at the time. "Guess it does."

In front of the mirror she set to rights all her careful disarray. I straightened my tie.

When we looked reasonably *soigné* again I said: "We'd better go upstairs and see what happened."

"Kids!" Caroline said bitterly. "I guess they fell asleep." She looked at me. "Anyway," she said, "you didn't suffer too, too much, did you?"

"As a matter of fact," I said, "I feel considerably refreshed after my forty winks. And it's now abundantly clear to me why fifty-nine point nine per cent of unmarried babies are born in the backs of cars."

"You've got it wrong," Caroline said; "it isn't the babies..."

"Never mind," I said. "Let's go!"

Upstairs we stopped outside Faraday's room and listened. Faraday's voice was saying: '... he suddenly caught hold of the goblin's other hand. He tied both hands together with rope. The goblin was a coward, and he fell on his knees at once...' "

I opened the door.

The twins were sitting up, wide-eyed, in Faraday's bed and the Neurologist himself was sitting cross-legged on the end of it, the orange, goblin-bedecked story-book in his hands.

"Uncle's reading us our new Noddy book," Peter said. "Go on, Uncle! What happened?"

"What happened to the goblin?" Penny said. "Tell us."

" 'Mercy! Don't take me away with you. Don't take me to Mr Plod. It was only a joke...!' "

"Talking of jokes," I interrupted. "What happened to our little arrangement, Peter?"

"I did! I did, Daddy," Peter said.

And Penny said: "I told Uncle I was firsty and look what he gave me. Peter's had some too. It's d'licious."

I looked. By the bedside was half a glass of beer.

"You haven't been giving that to my children?"

"Won't hurt them," Faraday said. "They just drank the froth. Now shall I finish the story or shall I not? It was getting exciting."

"You will not," I said. "Penny and Peter, go back to bed this minute."

And thus ended Caroline's Master Plan.

On the landing she said: "Thanks anyway," and went in after the twins.

The light was on in my bedroom. To my horror, I found Sylvia sitting up in bed.

I stared like an idiot.

"I thought you were out!" I said.

"So I gather!" Her voice was ominous.

"I didn't hear you come back."

"I gather that too."

I had to know if she had seen me with Caroline.

"When did you get in?"

"Nine-thirty."

"Are you sure?"

"Quite sure. Claudine wasn't feeling well, so I came home."

So that was that.

I decided that under the circumstances the truth was the best thing.

"If you saw me with Caroline," I began nonchalantly.

"If!" Sylvia said. "You couldn't have been less discreet. The door was wide open; and you were oblivious. Absolutely oblivious!"

"I must explain…" I said.

"You needn't bother…"

"You see," I said quickly. "Caroline wanted to do something quickly about Faraday, while he's here for the weekend, you see. So she thought that if he saw Caroline and me sort of…well, sort of…involved as you might say, he would become madly jealous and realise what he had been missing. I only did it as a favour to Caroline. It meant so little to me that I fell asleep in fact!"

"This is the end. The absolute end," Sylvia said as though I hadn't said a word. "I've heard of it happening but I must say I never thought it would happen to us. I suppose it's the seven-year-itch or something..."

"Eight..."

"...but I'm not going to be humiliated in my own house. I'm going back to mother on Monday."

"...why Monday? It's only Saturday night," I couldn't resist saying.

"She's away for the weekend." Her voice rose. "And what's more I'm taking the children and if anyone wants to know why..." She was shouting now.

"Sylvia, all the neighbours will hear," I whispered.

But she was really worked up. "Well, let them hear. Why shouldn't they know what a philandering, unfaithful, sex maniac I had the misfortune to marry? I should never have married you in the first place. I should have listened to Wilfred."

At the mention of her one-time, wealthy playboy fiancé I felt my good intentions of explanations disappearing and my gall rising.

"Don't you bring that miserable, impotent..."

"How dare you!"

"I suppose you know otherwise..." I leered, unforgivably.

"Don't be foul! You're just a throwback to your Uncle Albert. You *and* your precious Cousin Caroline."

Uncle Albert was the inevitable black sheep of our otherwise ordinary little family. He was a wealthy bachelor who lived on a farm in Winnipeg with what, as the story went, was an ever changing succession of succulent young ladies who stood the wide open spaces and Uncle Albert for just so long and then hopped it with the odd mink coat or diamond necklace, according to their length of stay.

"You know perfectly well this has nothing to do with Uncle Albert."

149

"Don't you be so sure. Uncle Albert must have got it from somewhere and you got it from Uncle Albert. Tarred with the same brush…"

I winced at the cliché.

"…and if you think it's the slightest bit funny…"

I decided to make one more attempt to explain.

"Sylvia, if you'd only listen!"

"What on earth is there to listen to? I come into my own house at a perfectly reasonable hour and find my own husband sprawled out on the sofa in the most disgusting…"

"Hey, wait a minute."

"Well, were you or were you not?"

"Were I not what?" I was really getting tangled up.

"Sprawled out?"

"Yes, of course I was sprawled out. You saw me. But the point is, if you'd only believe me, that it was all arranged beforehand. You can ask Caroline."

"I will not ask Caroline," Sylvia shouted and grabbed hold of her pillow. "You knew that I'd be out tonight! You've known since yesterday. When I think what I've done for that poor little misunderstood cousin of yours I could…"

"Sylvia!" I warned. But she had finished with words. She hurled the pillow with all her might at my head, stood up on the bed with the light of battle in her eyes and appeared to be about to jump on me.

Fortunately at that moment the telephone rang. Sylvia remained poised like an irate goddess.

"Phew!" I said from the floor where I had been knocked by the unexpected pillow. "Saved by the bell!"

It is common knowledge that in doctors' houses the ringing of the telephone is a pretty constant factor; it is not common knowledge that its urgent appeal can interrupt some of the most intimate moments of family life. It wasn't only that one couldn't eat, read or sleep in peace; one couldn't even have a decent slanging match with one's own wife without fear of interruption.

Like boxers at the end of a round we glared at each other and slunk into our corners; mine was by the telephone and Sylvia's in bed where she appropriated my pillow, hers being still on the floor where she had hurled it.

It was Gregg, Miss Chudley's maid, and she was almost incoherent with anxiety. Her beloved mistress had fallen down the stairs. I calmed her as best I could, told her not to try to move the old lady, and said that I would be over immediately.

With a quick glance in the mirror I tried in a moment to repair the damage of what were now two major battles in the course of what I had thought would be an ordinary Saturday evening, and dashed out.

It was midnight, and the house was in darkness, when I returned.

After the various *grandes drames* I had been through in the last few hours I felt limp, and hoped that Sylvia had got fed up with waiting for her opponent and fallen asleep.

I put the car away, took Billy for his nightly walk round the block and crept upstairs.

Her breathing was soft, slow and regular and I breathed a sigh of relief.

I got into bed quietly and, taking care not to bounce, lay as far away from Sylvia as I could. After a few moments I felt a warm foot reach out and touch my leg. I flinched away, thinking it was the prelude to a kick, and almost fell out of bed. The foot was followed by a hand and the hand by Sylvia who took me in her arms. I still didn't relax, unsure if it was really all right.

Then she said softly: "What was the matter with Miss Chudley?" and I knew that I had been forgiven.

Fifteen

In the morning, Sylvia, looking desirable, lying relaxed on her pillow watching me dress, said:

"You still haven't told me what was the matter with Miss Chudley."

I grinned. "You hardly gave me a chance."

Sylvia smiled. "You know, I really think you have something of Uncle Albert in you. In the nicest way of course."

"Of course."

She sighed. "Isn't it wonderful?"

"What?"

"Having a really good fight."

"It's a little wearing," I said.

"But it clears the air. I hope we never get too old."

"For what?"

"A good screech occasionally."

"You do understand? About Caroline."

"Of course. I knew all along there was nothing in it."

"Well, you might have told me last night," I said.

"Why on earth should I have?" Sylvia was smiling.

"Women!" I said, tying my tie.

"We have to have our fun," Sylvia said and turning over, promptly went back to sleep.

Miss Chudley had a fracture of the femur. It was an accident common among elderly people and one which frequently pre-cipitated the end of their lives. It wasn't the injury itself which brought about death. It was the fact that in order for the bone to mend it was necessary for the patient to have long bed-rest and this frequently led to respiratory complications and finally a fatal pneumonia. There were two ways of dealing with this not uncommon problem. One was to allow the injury to heal, as it would with time, unaided. The other was, by surgical intervention, to pin the fracture, thus enabling the patient to become mobile again more quickly. In the first case one took the risk of the effect of general anaesthesia on an elderly patient.

On Saturday night when a portable X-ray had confirmed the existence of a fracture, I had called in a physician to give an opinion as to whether Miss Chudley was a suitable candidate for operative treatment. He had found no contra-indication, apart from the general one of her advanced years, and this morning I was to discuss with her the question of the pinning of her femur.

Entering Miss Chudley's bedroom was like walking into the last century. There was rose-patterned wallpaper, a coal fire in the grate, bobbles on the curtains, green plush cloth on the table, marble-topped wash-stand, complete with china jug and basin, and a chamber-pot to match beneath the bed.

Miss Chudley, in her long-sleeved, white nightgown, lay flat in bed in considerable pain. Gregg, in shiny black dress, cap and apron, was in attendance.

"You're too good to me, Doctor," Miss Chudley said, smiling weakly, before I had said a word or done anything. "Gregg, something to warm the doctor, if you please."

Gregg slid silently out of the room and I knew she would return with a cut-glass decanter of sherry and one glass on a silver tray. It was useless to protest that I was not the slightest bit cold, that it was Sunday, my day off and that I was anxious to get home, that I detested sherry. Something to 'warm the doctor up' Miss Chudley had decreed and thus it would have to be.

I sipped my sherry, looking longingly at the green pot in which stood the green fern, but unfortunately it was too far away; also Gregg was watching. When I had finished and had come well out of the little exchange with Miss Chudley in which she insisted I take a second glass of the wretched stuff and I equally firmly refused, I suggested that we get down to business. I explained, as tactfully as I could, the situation, and waited apprehensively for the reaction I guessed would come when I suggested that Miss Chudley should undergo an operation. To my surprise she seemed not at all put out and said:

"If that's what you advise me to do, Doctor. I have absolute faith in you, as you know," and then she ruined it by saying: "The kitchen table is extremely large and Gregg, of course, can give it a good scrub."

"The kitchen table?"

"I think it will be quite suitable. Shall you administer the chloroform yourself?"

"Miss Chudley," I said.

"…Withers will hold me down, he's very strong, though of course I shall do my best not to struggle."

"But Miss Chudley!"

She held up a pale, ringed hand. "I know you will do your best: you always have."

This time I stood up. "Miss Chudley," I said sternly. "You must listen to me."

As gently as I could I explained about hospitals, surgeons and modern methods of anaesthesia. It took me almost an hour to talk Miss Chudley out of her ideas of kitchen-table surgery. I was almost hoarse by the time we reached a compromise. The compromise was this: Miss Chudley would agree to operation by the approved method, but there was to be no ambulance, Withers was to take her in the car, she would take her own sheets, towels and blankets with her, and the surgeon had, before he was allowed access to her femur, to be personally inspected by Miss Chudley herself.

The first two stipulations were not too difficult; the third needed a little thinking about. The surgeon whom I had originally intended to call in to operate on Miss Chudley was one whom I was sure, although the most competent man I knew, would not pass the first social hurdle. He was a forthright, North country man accustomed to speaking his thoughts; what his thoughts would be upon entering Miss Chudley's bedroom I shuddered to consider. The next on my list was a jolly Irishman who called everyone his 'darlin' girl'. I didn't think Miss Chudley would take kindly to the endearment. There was an excellent chap from my old hospital who firmly refused to speak to the patients at all, and a friend of Faraday's who treated all his patients, regardless of age, as though they were small children. I knew Miss Chudley would like neither being ignored nor having the site of operation referred to as her 'leggy-weggy'.

It was Sylvia who provided the solution to the problem. We were discussing it over lunch and by the time we reached dessert neither Faraday nor I had come up with anyone who was likely to be acceptable to Miss Chudley socially while at the same time having our confidence as a reliable surgeon. We had almost given up when Sylvia said: "What about Sir Arthur Colenutt?"

Faraday said: "Is he still alive?"

"As far as I know."

"Well, you'd better make sure, to be on the safe side," Faraday said ambiguously. But we knew that in the person of Sir Arthur, presuming he was still in the land of the living, lay the answer to our problem.

Sir Arthur Colenutt was a legend in his own time and since he belonged, in a way, to Miss Chudley's world, I didn't know why we hadn't thought of him before. He was a surgeon of international repute, whose skill, despite his years was much in demand, and while in the very vanguard of surgical progress still wore a morning-suit to consultations.

"Do you think I'll be able to get him?" I said doubtfully.

155

"Do you think she can afford him?" Faraday said.

"There's no question of that. Miss Chudley is rolling in it."

"Then all you can do is try."

"I'll ring him right away," I said, getting up from the table, and Sylvia said: "I hope you haven't forgotten we're taking the children out this afternoon."

I looked at her blankly trying to remember what, in a hasty moment, I had committed myself to.

"The Zoo," she said: "remember?"

"It all depends on Sir Arthur," I said. "If he wants to look at Miss Chudley this afternoon, then this afternoon it will have to be."

"On a Sunday?" Sylvia said. "He'll be having a snooze."

And as usual, she was right.

I had to use every wile I knew to get Sir Arthur to come to the telephone at all. His manservant had quite obviously dealt with importunate GPs such as myself, before. "No," he said. Sir Arthur was engaged. I visualised the roast beef and Yorkshire pudding. "No," he said politely, he had no idea when Sir Arthur would be disengaged. Of course, there'd be apple pie and custard and then most likely port and a cigar. Would I care to leave a message? To be mulled over, I supposed, before the post-prandial nap. I put all my cards on the table and explained to the manservant the nature of my problem with Miss Chudley. He agreed to discuss the matter with Sir Arthur if I would be kind enough to hold the line. My kindness had almost evaporated by the time that Sir Arthur, his mouth apparently still full of Yorkshire pudding, came to the telephone.

"Colenutt this end!"

I swallowed my cheeky riposte and announced my name.

"Dwy-knowyer?"

"No, I don't think you know me, sir, but I was wondering…"

"Meman's told me. Lady Budley, isn't it?"

"Miss Chudley!" I corrected.

"Not deaf, dear boy. Getting on; not deaf. All me faculties. Need 'em in my job. Ha-ha! Joking of course. Six o'clock all right? Must have me nap. Six o'clock eh?"

"That'll be fine," I said. "It's most kind of you."

"Not at all, dear boy. Surgical empyema, eh?"

"Fractured femur!"

"Wassat you say? Shockin' line. Don't trouble. We'll soon have him on his feet. 'Bye, dear boy."

"Goodbye," I sighed to the dialling tone.

"Are you sure he's all right?" I said to Faraday. "He sounded half daft to me."

"It's his act," Faraday said. "He's used that gimmick since he was an HP in the year dot. Jolly bright of him to have thought of it. Look where it's got him. Knighthood, surgeon to royalty..."

"Can he really hear, though?"

"Better than you can. It's an idea..."

"What?"

"Acting barmy. And mucking about in a tail-coat. Think of a gimmick for me."

"Just be yourself," Sylvia said; "they might lock you up yet."

"Well," I said to Sylvia expansively, "I am yours until six o'clock. Are you coming with us, Caroline?"

"Am I just! If there's one thing I get a kick out of it's all those quaint little animals."

"What, *all* my pretty ones?" Faraday said. "I was hoping some kind soul would give me a hand."

"Doing what?"

"I have about three acres of notes to type out for the Neurological Society. I'm reading a paper. With my one finger it will take from now until Doomsday."

Caroline stopped dead in her tracks on the way to the door. "Well," she said, "I guess I could go to the Zoo any old time."

Sitting on a bench in the Zoo with Sylvia while we watched the twins ecstatically feed bread to the antelopes, I said: "Do you realise we're behaving like normal people?"

"How do you mean?"

"How long is it since we've taken the children out like this?"

Sylvia thought. "I can't remember."

"Neither can I."

Of course it was all thanks to Robin who was a tremendous asset in the practice. I felt that a great impossible-to-bear weight had been lifted from my shoulders, and I had every reason to congratulate myself on my choice of assistant. There was enough work to keep us both occupied and Robin couldn't understand how I had once managed to get through it all single-handed. Now, I scarcely understood myself. Having slowed down and become accustomed to work at a normal pace it was difficult to imagine how I had ever wound myself up to the ridiculous extent that I never walked when I could run, never used three words when two would do, and unwittingly turned the patients who came to consult me into quivering jellies for whom I probably prescribed sedatives. Now that I had someone to help me, I could allow the patients to talk freely, and was able to listen without that too-familiar feeling of almost unbearable irritability creeping up to engulf me as I envisaged the packed waiting-room beyond. I no longer grew almost hysterical when people flooded in three minutes before the end of surgery, and merely by listening to what they had to say I discovered amazing things about my patients that I had simply not had time to elicit before. Only at meal-times did the old order, by force of incorrigible habit, persist. As the head of the house I was, of course, served first. By the time Sylvia, Caroline and the children had picked up their forks to begin, I was gnashing my teeth at an empty plate. Try as I would it was impossible for me to eat more slowly; neither had I the patience to sit and watch while the rest of the family transferred the food from plates to mouths with what seemed to me, deliberate sluggishness. There was no socially acceptable solution. So, as the mood took me, I sat and glared; made a few telephone calls in the interval; read the newspaper, or demanded that the dessert be brought forthwith.

In the practice, Robin was slowly building up his own clientele. At first some of the patients had imagined that we were rival organisations and shamefacedly confessed to me that they had consulted Robin in my absence. It hadn't taken long though for the new arrangement to get over its teething troubles. Robin's face had now become familiar in the waiting-room and on the doorstep, and the patients were grateful that they no longer had to wait an unreasonable length of time before being seen. During my new-found hours of leisure, even my most regular 'regulars' were quite happy to take their troubles to Robin and many of them commented on how foolish I had been not to share my burden before. Perhaps they didn't realise that in addition to my burden I was now sharing a large portion of my income, but I would not now have it any other way.

"This is the life!" I said, as a gust of wind blowing directly across from the rodent house reminded me where I was.

"Just look at Peter's socks," Sylvia said.

"What's the matter with them?"

"They're round his ankles."

"Where do you expect a small boy's socks to be?"

"And Penny's face! She keeps running her hands along the railings then rubbing them on her face."

"They're happy." I watched them holding half-nervous palms scattered with bread to the nuzzling mouths of the antelopes. "So am I."

And it was true. It was about the first Sunday afternoon since our marriage that I had spent just being a 'Dad', and there was nothing like it. We lingered in the echoing lion house and admired the jungle kings, secure in the knowledge that renal colics, threatened abortions and other Sunday afternoon emergencies would be more than adequately dealt with by Robin. We tried to throw cabbages into the gaping maws of the rhinoceroses and lost them in the steamy, stinking water, unfettered by the fact that at home the telephone might be, and probably was, ringing.

Peter rode on the elephant, assuring us that it had been 'super' when we lifted him down pale-faced with apprehension, and Penny, less adventurous, made friends with a matted nanny-goat in the Children's Corner. We ate peanuts intended for the monkeys, ice-lollies in the cold March wind and had tea at a smeary, tea-slopped counter which I'm sure the twins thought was the Ritz.

At six o'clock I left Sylvia and two blissfully happy, weary, filthy children at home, and went round to Miss Chudley's for my consultation with Sir Arthur Colenutt.

He had beaten me to it. Outside Miss Chudley's house was a Rolls-Royce, older and squarer even than Miss Chudley's own, in which was a sleeping chauffeur.

The scene into which I stepped, feeling like an intruder from Mars, was pure Dickens. Miss Chudley, surrounded by her ferns and knick-knacks was gazing with admiration upon Sir Arthur who sat in his morning-coat, winged-collar and spats, by her bedside, taking snuff from a silver box.

"Ah, Doctor!" Miss Chudley said. "Do come in. Sir Arthur was just telling me that he knew my poor sister Grace."

"Very well! Very well indeed!" Sir Arthur said, lifting the snuff to his purple nose. "Henley before the war. Charmin' too. Charmin'!"

"I remember my father taking me to Henley before the war," I said. "Of course I was a small boy at the time."

Sir Arthur took out his monocle, screwed it into his eye and looked at me deprecatingly.

"Not *that* war, dear boy, *our* war, eh, Miss Chudley? The 'Pack up your Troubles' war. Grace Chudley? Of course I remember her, dear lady. What happened to her?"

"Heart," Miss Chudley said. "She was eighty-four when the Almighty took her. Poor Grace was never very strong."

Sir Arthur seemed about to say something when he drew his knees up to his chest, dropped his monocle from his eye and began to twitch in the most alarming fashion, at the same time becoming more and more purple.

"God," I thought, "the old boy's having a fit." I was just about to rush to his aid when he whipped from his pocket a snuff-coloured handkerchief and sneezed into it the most gargantuan sneeze I had ever heard.

Miss Chudley nodded approvingly. "And again," she said, "and again."

When Sir Arthur had resumed his normal colour and composure and had put away his handkerchief, Miss Chudley about whom I had been wondering if she had missed her cue, said: "Gregg, what about a little something to warm the gentlemen?" but Sir Arthur, more daring than I, held up a peremptory hand.

"First things first, dear lady. First things first." He shuffled his chair nearer to the bed and said coaxingly: "Let's first have a look at this old empyema of yours."

"Fractured femur," I said softly.

Sir Arthur spun round. "Young man," he said, "don't teach your grandmother to suck eggs!"

Under the spell of Sir Arthur, who had known her sister Grace, Miss Chudley agreed to go into a private nursing home, where, he assured her, she would be looked after like old china, for operation.

We fixed the date for Tuesday, giving Miss Chudley a full day to settle down in St Hilda's. Sir Arthur refused my offer to assist at the operation, pointing out that he always worked with his own team, but promised to ring me as soon as he had finished.

The matter having been settled to the satisfaction of us all, Sir Arthur, rubbing his hands in anticipation, declared himself

161

ready for the traditional glass, only in his case it turned out to be glasses.

I left him reminiscing over the sherry with Miss Chudley and went home to recuperate from my afternoon among the birds and beasts.

Sixteen

"It's humiliating," Caroline said on Sunday night when Faraday had gone; "I guess I'll go back to the States."

"What happened this afternoon then? You had long enough alone together."

"Nothing," Caroline said. "Precisely nothing except that I typed my fingers to the bone and I know now a lot more about the cases of dysarthria than I did before."

"Look," I said, hating to see her so depressed. "Would you like me to say something to Faraday? In a roundabout way of course; I'd be terribly tactful."

Caroline shook her head. "If a guy can't see when a girl's crazy about him he must be awful disinterested."

"Or have other things on his mind," I said in Faraday's defence. "He left in a bit of a hurry, didn't he?"

"He couldn't wait to get back to a cranio-pharyngyoma. That's how fascinating he found me."

"I'm sorry to say this," I said, "but I honestly think that as far as Faraday's concerned you're wasting your time. In my opinion he's a born bachelor. He lives, thinks and dreams medicine and has as long as I've known him. Which, of course, is why he has got where he is."

"What a terrible waste!" Caroline sighed and we left it, for the moment, at that.

I felt sorry for Caroline. Since the fire at the school she hadn't been the same girl. She not only seemed to have lost interest in her teenagers and their Sex habits, but also in her diet and her calory intake and frequently forgot to take her tablets. Even the children noticed the change. Cousin Caroline, Penny said, no longer seemed to care for Noddy and his adventures and she seemed to have exhausted, according to Peter, her seemingly bottomless stock of cowboy yarns. She wasn't, they declared unanimously, 'fun' any longer.

Sylvia and I were worried.

"Perhaps I should have a word with Faraday," Sylvia said on Tuesday afternoon when Caroline, who hadn't strayed far from the telephone since Sunday night, had given up hope of a call from Faraday.

"How would that help?"

"Well, the feminine touch; I could throw out a few hints."

"You can lead a horse to water..." I said sagely. "He saw enough of Caroline over the weekend."

"Nevertheless, I think I'll try. I hate to see her so depressed."

"You women," I said, "just love meddling."

"If we didn't give you a shove now and again most of you would never get married. You innocent males don't realise how much undercover work goes on."

"Ha!" I said. "If Faraday isn't interested in Caroline there's nothing you or I or anyone else can do about it. It's as simple as that."

"I wouldn't be so sure," Sylvia said.

I thought for a moment. "No one had to 'undercover' me into wanting to marry you. I remember you now at the Hospital Dance in that scarlet dress with your hair on top of your head when I decided you were the only girl for me."

"Have I changed much?"

I looked at Sylvia in her skirt and jumper and flat-heeled shoes sewing a button on Peter's grey school shirt.

"Yes."

"In what way?"

"You look a real doctor's wife."

"Thanks!"

"It was intended as a compliment."

Sylvia looked up from her mending. "I suppose now that the children are at school all day," she said thoughtfully, "and Maria can answer the telephone I *could* go back to modelling."

"Would you like to?"

"Going to work in the rush hour," Sylvia said, "standing for fittings, aching, aching feet, smiling when you don't feel in the least bit like it, so many beautiful clothes all day that you grow to hate them. No."

"You prefer the telephone and the doorbell, and the disturbed nights and people's complaints, and the lack of privacy and peace, and the children and the endless procession of Miss Winterhalters and Marias..."

"...and the gory accidents that always happen when you're out, and the specimen bottles decorating the hall table, and the way the patients take it out on me when you aren't instantly available..."

"...and the hundredweights of advertisements cluttering the house and the drug travellers calling at the door..."

"...and the Consultants when you're spring-cleaning and have nowhere to put them, and babies being sick in the waiting-room..."

"Well?"

"Yes," Sylvia said. "I prefer it."

"I wonder why?"

Sylvia looked at me. "Because I love you and it's part of you."

"Even Mrs Bridgewater's veins?" I said; they had now become a standing joke.

Sylvia nodded. "Even Mrs Bridgewater's veins. You've been at it too long. You can't detach yourself."

"I don't know that I want to, now that I've got Robin to help me."

"You couldn't anyway, it's too late."

"If you'd married Wilfred," I said, thinking of Sylvia's former fiancé, "you wouldn't have been so tired sometimes that by the end of the day you could hardly stagger."

"I would rather be tired," Sylvia said clearly, "from helping you cope with measles and mumps, and broken heads and broken legs, and insect bites and miscarriages in the night and hysterics in the day, than tired from Ascot and Wimbledon and trailing from Scotland to Monte Carlo and Monte Carlo to Scotland."

"In that case," I said, "I feel compelled to kiss you."

"Dowdy as I am?"

"Did I say dowdy?"

"You said I'd changed."

"The change was for the better."

When I released her Sylvia said: "I'm going to phone Faraday. Where will he be?"

"In his consulting rooms. He's seeing a patient of mine today. Be tactful, Sweetie..." But Sylvia had gone.

When she came back she looked gloomy.

"So much for the undercover work," I said.

"I just couldn't get him interested. He kept talking about a treatment for hydrocephalus he was working on."

"Did he say anything about the patient I sent him?"

"Yes. She was due half an hour ago but hadn't turned up."

"Odd," I said, "that's not like Mrs Rowbottom."

But I had no time to ponder any longer on Mrs Rowbottom's failure to keep her appointment with Faraday for just then there was an urgent knocking at the morning-room door and work once again banished domestic problems from my head.

It was Robin. There was an urgent call, he said, from Mrs MacConnal, and would I like him to go? I told him that I'd go myself since I had always dealt with her, and instantly all thoughts of Caroline's ill-fated romance, together with a load of trivia, vanished from my head.

It wasn't like Mrs MacConnal to call me in the daytime. When I arrived at the filthy flat I found the circumstances not the same either.

I found the children half-dressed playing marbles on the floor of the bedroom, MacConnal gazing idly out of the window waiting for opening time, the air heavy as usual with a hundred repugnant smells, and Mrs MacConnal sitting up in bed fighting for her life. The difference was that this time it seemed unlikely she would win.

She was as grey as her sordid sheets, had ice-cold extremities and the clamminess of death on her skin. My stethoscope, echoing with her rapid, stertorous breathing, confirmed my first impression. Her chest was filled with fluid in which this time there was little I could do to stop her drowning.

I gave her some morphia and shouted at MacConnal to go down to my car and bring up the small cylinder of oxygen I kept in the boot for emergencies such as this. When he was at the door I said: "You'd better leave the children with a neighbour."

He looked at me enquiringly for I'd never before made such a suggestion, and what he found in my face made him take hold of a child in each hand, tuck another under his arm and actually run for the door.

By the time he returned, a great, wasted hulk of a man carrying the heavy cylinder as though it were a child's balloon, Mrs MacConnal, too weak to sit up and ease her chest any longer, was lying flat and taking the last of her tortured breaths.

Without the children the room seemed quiet and the breathing, though less noisy than it had been, filled every corner. She was past help from the oxygen, past help from anyone or anything. The breathing, like a clockwork motor for which there was no key, grew weaker, fainter, and finally died away. With the unaccustomed silence, MacConnal and I became aware of each other's presence. He looked his question at me bent over my stethoscope, and received his answer when I folded it slowly and put it in my pocket.

I never thought the time would come when I would feel pity for a drunken, shiftless, idle lump of humanity like MacConnal but as he made for the door of the bedroom I saw tears in the bloodshot eyes.

"Where are you going?" I said, but looking at my watch I knew what the answer was. It was five minutes to opening time.

I made some arrangements with the neighbours, aware that MacConnal would be out for the count until morning and, depressed, set off for home and my Evening Surgery.

I hated to lose patients, and with the Reverend Barker the score was now two deaths in the past few months. It was common knowledge that in General Practice these things happened in cycles of three. I hoped that this time the uncanny rule would prove wrong and though I tried hard to concentrate on who would now care for the poor little MacConnals and not upon death, I arrived home with a horrid sense of foreboding.

Just as the demands of the practice often pre-empted domestic matters from my head, so one patient would cause me for the moment to forget all anxiety concerning a previous one.

My first patient in the Evening Surgery was Mrs Rowbottom, and I thought that she was going to hit me.

All I did was to sit down at my desk and press my buzzer when the door to the waiting-room opened as if struck by a tornado and Mrs Rowbottom advanced on me like a knight in armour, her umbrella as her sword.

I stood up alarmed; the end of her umbrella had a nasty-looking point on it.

"My dear Mrs Rowbottom," I said, and grasped the ferrule just in time.

"Don't you 'dear Mrs Rowbottom' me!" she said, struggling to pull it away.

I held fast, thus ensuring that she kept at least an umbrella length away.

"I've come to tell you exactly what I think of you..." Mrs Rowbottom said.

I let go of the umbrella. "Well, if you don't mind, I'll just close the waiting-room door."

"As far as I'm concerned," Mrs Rowbottom said, as I made sure the soundproof door was firmly closed, "the more people who hear what I have to say the better. Why shouldn't they all know what an incompetent pip-squeak..."

I nipped round behind the bastion of my desk and held up my hand to the lady who was quivering from head to foot.

"Look, Mrs Rowbottom, won't you sit down and let me hear what you have to say quietly?"

To my relief she lowered her umbrella and perched herself on the very edge of the chair.

I suddenly remembered. Mrs Rowbottom was supposed to have seen Faraday. I wondered what on earth he had done to upset her.

"I suppose," I said, "you've just been to see Doctor Faraday..."

"No, I have not!"

"Your appointment was for this afternoon, was it not?"

"It most certainly was."

"Then why didn't you keep it? Doctor Faraday's a very busy man, you know; one of our most eminent Neurologists..."

"Why? Why? Why?" Mrs Rowbottom's voice was becoming hysterical and I doubted that my soundproof door could withstand such assault. "I'll tell you why, young man! I'll tell you why, you cocky little upstart." She was fumbling in her handbag almost blind with rage. "*This* is why!"

In a trembling hand she held out a letter. I recognised the envelope as one of my own and the handwriting to be mine. It was the letter of introduction I had written for Mrs Rowbottom to make to Faraday. My heart sank just a little but there was still hope.

I took the envelope and turned it over. It had been steamed open. I began to feel queasy. Mrs Rowbottom was looking at me triumphantly. Because there was not a thing for the moment

169

that I could think of to say, I removed the letter I had written from the envelope.

'*Chère Confrère*,' it said,
'Herewith one Mrs Rowbottom. This lady purports to be suffering from no less than thirty-two symptoms; to name but a few: palpitations, headache, inertia, sweating, giddiness, nausea, wind, itching, numbness of various limbs, nightmares, insomnia, spots before the eyes, loss of appetite, pain in abdomen, head, ear, eye, chest, knee, elbow and great toe.

Sort this one out if you can. At least it will give you something to pass away the idle hours, and she can well afford it.

As far as I am concerned, Mrs Rowbottom is an exceptionally healthy specimen of forty-one years, and it is my considered opinion that all that is wrong with her is that she has too much money and is bored with her husband.

Don't say I'm not trying.

Your Partner in Crime…'

I decided to try to bluff it out.

"Mrs Rowbottom," I said sternly, "are you aware that this letter is not addressed to you?"

"Perfectly."

"Then it was hardly ethical of you, was it, to…"

"Ethical!" she screamed. "You talk to me of ethics! I shall report you for this! Report you to the highest medical authorities. I shall see to it personally that you are struck off…"
You could have heard her in the next street.

She was still screaming when Robin put his head round the door.

"Sorry to interrupt," he said, "but can you take a call from St Hilda's Nursing Home?"

I knew it would be Sir Arthur Colenutt about Miss Chudley and that I wouldn't be able to hear a thing with Mrs Rowbottom shouting.

"I'll take it outside," I said. "Excuse me one moment, Mrs Rowbottom."

In the hall, Sylvia was watering her plants and Robin searching for something in his case.

After I'd taken the call and replaced the receiver I stood thinking for a moment, and Sylvia said: "Is anything the matter?"

I watched her pull off a yellowed leaf.

"It's Miss Chudley," I said. "Pulmonary embolism. She's dead."

Robin looked at me. "Anything I can do?"

"Yes, get rid of Mrs Rowbottom, there's a good chap."

Seventeen

"Do you think they'll give us the money straight away?" Sylvia said. She was referring to our inheritance.

For a week after Miss Chudley's death which had been as much of a shock to Sir Arthur as it had to myself, the old lady had seemed in such good shape, I had felt utterly depressed. With the deaths of the Reverend Barker, Mrs MacConnal and Miss Chudley I had lost, all within a short space of time, three of my 'old stagers'; three of the constants as it were, to whom I had become accustomed and around whom the changing legions of my large list of patients revolved facelessly. I was like a head-master whose sixth form had left, faced with the task of making new prefects. Who now would be my spiritual mentor, who my eccentric, who the regular disrupter of my nights? Like them, love them, pity them, hate them, running at various times the whole gamut of emotions, the patients were, in the final analysis, my *raison d'être*. Their loss was ultimately mine.

It was on the Monday week after Miss Chudley's death that we heard from her solicitor, one Isaiah Bailey, that his client, just as she had promised, had left me something in her will. The exact extent of the bequest Mr Bailey was not in a position to tell me until the following Thursday when he requested that I call upon him at his office.

At first I had been unmoved, mentioning it only casually to Sylvia, my mind on other things.

Sylvia, however, took it differently. "Sweetie!" she said excitedly, "don't you see, we shall be able to make an offer for the farm."

"How do you know how much it will be?"

"Well, you did say Miss Chudley was terribly wealthy."

"True. But anyway if it is anything more than a small gift I couldn't possibly accept it."

"Why not?"

"I didn't do anything for her."

"But that's beside the point. This isn't for services rendered and she did think an awful lot of you. You were, after all, her Saint."

"Look, Sweetie," I said. "Let's say no more about it. I suggest we wait until Thursday when we see Mr Bailey."

But between Monday and Thursday, against my better judgement, a subtle change took place, engendered, I suppose, by a further look at the farm we had on Tuesday, the flames fanned by Sylvia's enthusiasm.

The house which we now referred to as 'our house', had been newly pink-washed; the hedges were sprouting and the orchards in pastel blossom. Deep in mud, the property had looked desirable, now it looked like anybody's dream house, and even I could not help the odd speculative thought upon the generosity of Miss Chudley.

By the time Thursday arrived, Sylvia and I in our fertile imaginations must have spent some fifty thousand pounds. We not only bought the farm, we redecorated it throughout, laid Aubusson carpets on the floors and in the drive set a 300 SL Mercedes for Sylvia and a dignified Rolls-Bentley for me. Naturally in the paddock there was a well-behaved pony for Peter and an equally good-mannered one for Penny; the groom and the stable-boy doffed their caps each time they saw me.

On Thursday, as we climbed the dusty stairs to the solicitor's office, I answered Sylvia's question.

"No," I said, "of course they won't give us the money straight away."

Mr Bailey obviously belonged to the Club. Like Miss Chudley and Sir Arthur Colenutt, his was an age gone by. The room in which we waited, hearts thumping with anticipation, was gloomy, decorated with sporting prints and indescribably dreary. The clerk who ushered us into the presence, was gloomier and more dreary still. Mr Bailey himself was like an ancient bird whose glasses slid constantly down his beak.

"I won't keep you long, Doctor," he said, his little voice coming from a small, pursed mouth. "I know how busy you must be."

"Never too busy for good news," I said heartily.

He looked at me sharply through his glasses, then again over the tops of them.

"Well," he said, clutching tremblingly at some papers on his desk until he captured the one he wanted. "I have before me the last Will and Testament of my good friend, the late Miss Amelia Agnes Lettice Chudley, gone to her eternal rest."

I bowed my head.

Mr Bailey shunted his spectacles up his nose. "The said Miss Amelia Agnes Lettice Chudley…" his voice tailed off and he read over the first two pages of the will to himself in a bumbling mutter from which we could distinguish nothing. Suddenly he stopped and jabbed at the document with a lumpy finger. "Ah!"

Sylvia and I sat forward.

Mr Bailey looked at us for a moment then down again at the document.

" 'To my doctor,' " he said, quoting, " 'a true Saint and Nobleman,' " I lowered my eyes modestly, " 'I bequeath the sum of twenty-five thousand pounds…' "

I grabbed Sylvia's hand. We didn't listen to the rest. Against a background of Mr Bailey's arid voice we were busy laying the Aubusson carpets.

Twenty-five thousand pounds! So the old girl really had meant it. Wherever she was, I took off my hat to her.

Mr Bailey was folding the will and replacing it in a buff envelope.

He looked at us. "I hope you understand, Doctor, that the reason I asked you to come here today was because it was my duty, as the Executor of the Estate of my good friend the late Miss Amelia Agnes Lettice Chudley, to inform you of her wishes as laid down in her last Will and Testament and duly signed and witnessed."

"Of course," I said: "I understand."

Mr Bailey removed his glasses completely. Without them he still looked like a bird but a naked one.

"Doctor," he said, leaning forward. "I don't think you do understand."

"Why not?" I asked, losing patience with the tedious old man and itching to get outside alone with Sylvia to discuss our good fortune.

"Because," he said, each word an entity, "there is *no Estate* to administer."

I wasn't with him.

"In her will," Mr Bailey continued, "the late Miss Chudley left you, in appreciation of your services and many kindnesses to her, the sum of twenty-five thousand pounds. The other Executors and myself have been most thoroughly into the matter and it appears that, let alone the twenty-five thousand pounds she willed to you, the good lady, when she passed on, did not possess even twenty-five pence. Her debts were phenomenal. Quite, quite phenomenal!"

"But what about the Castle in Scotland, the London properties, the Cornish Village?" I said.

Mr Bailey replaced his glasses, leaned forward across his desk and looked at me as though I were a small child.

175

"Doctor," he said and, fascinated, I watched his Adam's apple appear over his wing-collar, "have you never seen delusions of grandeur?"

Of course I should have suspected it; Miss Chudley's manner, the outdated set-up which she insisted upon maintaining, the frequent allusions to her fortune. It was one big play-act and I, among others, was the dupe.

We went down the dusty stairs more slowly than we had gone up. On the journey home neither of us spoke, each occupied with fading visions of large houses, bottled plums and the squeal of piglets.

At home we found Faraday sitting gloomily in the morning-room watching the twins play Snap. Sylvia went to make some tea.

"What's up with you?" I said to Faraday because it was unusual to see him in the middle of an afternoon on a working day. "Have they given you the sack?"

"Don't joke," Faraday said in a mournful voice. "I'm ill."

I was in no mood myself to toss the hoary old 'Why don't you see a doctor?' tag into his lap. And anyway he really didn't look too good.

"What's the trouble?"

Faraday scratched his head. "I don't know. The symptoms don't seem to fit in with anything I've ever heard of. That's why I thought I'd pop over."

"What are they?"

"Loss of appetite," he said; "I just can't seem to get interested in food at all, loss of weight, insomnia – I toss and turn all night – inability to concentrate, weakness of the limbs – I drop everything I pick up – vagueness, amnesia… I'm getting rather worried. I can't do my work properly."

"How long has this been going on?"

Faraday thought. "Nearly two weeks."

I did a small calculation in my head.

"It started soon after you stayed here for the weekend."

"Yes. Yes, I suppose it did. You don't think it's anything serious?"

"Well, fairly," I said.

He looked alarmed. "Not early disseminated sclerosis or a partial lobe tumour?"

"No," I said, "not anything like that."

"What then?"

"You," I said, "are presenting a syndrome common to young adult males but most usually appearing between the ages of eighteen and twenty-five."

"I've been all through Cecil and Price," Faraday said, mentioning the two best-known medical textbooks, "and I couldn't find anything that really applied."

"I'm not surprised," I said. "You have one of the diseases most common to mankind. You, my dear fellow, are in love!"

"In love?"

"With Caroline. It all fits in, date of onset…"

"With Caroline?"

"Caroline."

"Odd you should mention her."

"How, odd?"

"Well, I forgot to tell you this bit, but every time I read over my notes for the Paper I'm presenting at the meeting next week I can't see a word. You know why?"

"No."

"Because on every page all I can see is Caroline's face, her eyes, her mouth, smiling at me…"

"They were the notes she typed for you?"

"Yes, but…"

"My dear boy," I said, "it's fortunate that the complaint you have, while serious, is not incurable. The treatment is simple. Penny," I said; "where's your Cousin Caroline?"

"Out. Snap!" she yelled, throwing down a card.

"Gone to buy her ticket," Peter said.

177

"She's going back to Ermerica," Penny added. "She's going to send me a postcard."

"Look, you just lie back in that chair," I said to Faraday, "and don't move."

"Perhaps a little shock therapy?" Faraday suggested.

"Now keep calm," I said. "I don't want you to worry about a thing. I'll be back shortly."

In the kitchen, Caroline, having just come in, was watching Sylvia prepare tea.

"Gosh, Doc," she said when she saw me. "I'm awful sorry."

"What about?"

"The inheritance. Not a nickel! Sylvia just told me. All that fabulous blossom and that darling house! How could she do such a thing! Couldn't you spit!"

"We'll get over it," I said. "Look, Caroline?"

"Ugh?"

I looked wildly round the kitchen and my glance fell on two pink blancmanges Sylvia had put out for the children's tea. I picked them up. "Take these into the morning-room for the twins, there's a good girl!"

"But, Sweetie!" Sylvia said, looking at Caroline standing there in her smart navy-blue suit holding the blancmanges, "you know the children have their tea in the kitchen."

I drew myself up to my full impressive height. "I," I said impressively, "am the boss. Caroline, the blancmange!"

Half an hour later we crept into the morning-room.

Faraday was sitting in the armchair where I had left him. Caroline, gazing into his eyes, was on his lap. On the floor, Penny and Peter, their game forgotten, sat cross-legged, transfixed as before the television. Penny held a finger to her lips. "Ssh!" she said. "Daddy, look at Cousin Caroline!"

Cousin Caroline was stroking Faraday's hair.

"Well," I said to Faraday, "how was my diagnosis?"

He didn't take his eyes off Caroline. "Spot-on," he said, "as usual. What about the treatment?"

"You have it," I said, "on your knee."

"Is it a permanent cure?"

"The only one there is, I'm afraid, for this particular complaint."

"It's the most beautiful medicine I've seen," Faraday said, looking at Caroline.

"Cousin Caroline," Penny said; "what will be on the postcard?"

"Wedding bells?" Faraday said, raising his eyebrows questioningly at Caroline.

"You just bet!" she breathed and buried her face in his.

Sylvia, a twin in each hand, crept out of the room. Feeling my presence superfluous to the occasion I followed her into the kitchen.

"Well!" Sylvia said when the twins were sitting at the table, "all in all it's been quite a day."

I knew she was thinking about the farm.

"I can't say it's not a shame," I said. "I could just picture that extra line in my obituary, 'sorely missed by his chickens and pigs.' "

"People shed better tears," Sylvia said by way of consolation. People!

I thought of Miss Chudley, Mrs MacConnal and the Reverend Barker who were dead, and Mrs Theobald, Mrs Bridgewater, Mr Adams, Miss Gibbs and a thousand other patients to whom I couldn't put names, who lived. It was an endless cavalcade and in it, quite clearly and with love, I saw my destiny.

I knew where I was going.

ROSEMARY FRIEDMAN

GOLDEN BOY

This is one of Rosemary Friedman's best-loved novels. Freddie Lomax is a slick, work-driven city executive, popular and sociable, other eyes always drawn to the magnetic field of his charm. Utterly without warning he is given two hours to clear his desk at the bank and he finds himself joining the ranks of the middle-aged unemployed. His confidence that a new job will appear proves unfounded, and with all the time he now spends at home his marriage to Jane begins to suffer...until, when he thinks he can go no lower, he discovers that he is not the only one with problems and he applies his talents to a last attempt to save his relationship.

'What a story! What a storyteller!' *Daily Mail*

LIFE SITUATION

Oscar John has it all: a successful author, he has been married happily for sixteen years. But then everything changes when he meets Marie-Céleste, an elegant French doctor. When his sexual curiosity turns into passion and an all-consuming love, he is completely unprepared...

ROSEMARY FRIEDMAN

PROOFS OF AFFECTION

One year in the life of a London Jewish family at a time of great change: Sydney Shelton's business is not doing too well these days, but he has provided for his future and his worries are not about trade but about his own health and his children, now young adults. Sydney's wife Kitty knows how ill he is – but they cannot talk about it. The children openly flout tradition and go against his wishes. What will happen to them if he dies?

With a light satirical touch and great sensitivity, Rosemary Friedman explores the tensions and deeper feelings of a traditional family facing the pressures of change in a non-religious society. A thoughtful and moving novel.

ROSE OF JERICHO

Kitty's husband Sydney is dead, and eighteen months later she is still struggling to come to terms with his death. She takes comfort in the lives of her children, and the full comedy and crises of Kitty's circle of family and friends vividly unfold. On a package holiday to Israel, in between awe-inspiring visits to the Dead Sea and the dramatic desert, she gets to know Maurice Morgenthau, reserved New Yorker and survivor of the Nazi concentration camps. The friendship between them grows and Maurice helps Kitty gain a new sense of perspective on her life. In turn Kitty helps Maurice tell his harrowing story of survival for the first time.

Rosemary Friedman

To Live in Peace

This novel pursues the story of widow Kitty Sheldon from Rosemary Friedman's delightful earlier novels *Proofs of Affection* and *Rose of Jericho*. Kitty has watched her beloved husband die, and her children grow to adulthood. She takes security from her role as family matriarch, but now her north London Jewish community is rife with dispute about the recent Israeli invasion of Lebanon. At the invitation of her gentlemanly suitor, Holocaust survivor Maurice Morgenthau, Kitty visits New York – where she learns to please herself and in so doing learns to *discover* herself too.

Vintage

Clare de Cluzac seems to have it all she could ever want – but underneath her confident exterior lie the scars of an emotionally brutalised childhood. When her authoritarian, philandering father threatens to sell the family château and vineyards, Clare takes a big risk and flies to Bordeaux to run them herself, even though she will have to learn everything from scratch.

As she fights to overcome the many obstacles placed (often deliberately) in her way, she confronts old ghosts and grows into her new role as the *chatelaine* – discovering on the way new knowledge and a deeper understanding of her own desires.

OTHER TITLES BY ROSEMARY FRIEDMAN AVAILABLE DIRECT
FROM HOUSE OF STRATUS

Quantity		£	$(US)	$(CAN)	€
☐	THE COMMONPLACE DAY	6.99	11.50	15.99	11.50
☐	AN ELIGIBLE MAN	6.99	11.50	15.99	11.50
☐	THE FRATERNITY	6.99	11.50	15.99	11.50
☐	THE GENERAL PRACTICE	6.99	11.50	15.99	11.50
☐	GOLDEN BOY	6.99	11.50	15.99	11.50
☐	INTENSIVE CARE	10.99	17.99	26.95	18.00
☐	THE LIFE SITUATION	6.99	11.50	15.99	11.50
☐	LONG HOT SUMMER	6.99	11.50	15.99	11.50
☐	LOVE ON MY LIST	6.99	11.50	15.99	11.50
☐	A LOVING MISTRESS	6.99	11.50	15.99	11.50
☐	NO WHITE COAT	6.99	11.50	15.99	11.50
☐	PRACTICE MAKES PERFECT	6.99	11.50	15.99	11.50
☐	PROOFS OF AFFECTION	6.99	11.50	15.99	11.50
☐	ROSE OF JERICHO	6.99	11.50	15.99	11.50
☐	A SECOND WIFE	6.99	11.50	15.99	11.50
☐	TO LIVE IN PEACE	6.99	11.50	15.99	11.50
☐	VINTAGE	6.99	11.50	15.99	11.50
☐	WE ALL FALL DOWN	6.99	11.50	15.99	11.50

ALL HOUSE OF STRATUS BOOKS ARE AVAILABLE FROM GOOD BOOKSHOPS
OR DIRECT FROM THE PUBLISHER:

Internet: www.houseofstratus.com including author interviews, reviews, features.

Email: sales@houseofstratus.com please quote author, title, and credit card details.

Hotline: UK ONLY: 0800 169 1780, please quote author, title and credit card details.
INTERNATIONAL: +44 (0) 20 7494 6400, please quote author, title, and credit card details.

Send to: House of Stratus Sales Department
24c Old Burlington Street
London
W1X 1RL
UK

Please allow for postage costs charged per order plus an amount per book as set out in the tables below:

	£(Sterling)	$(US)	$(CAN)	€(Euros)
Cost per order				
UK	2.00	3.00	4.50	3.30
Europe	3.00	4.50	6.75	5.00
North America	3.00	4.50	6.75	5.00
Rest of World	3.00	4.50	6.75	5.00
Additional cost per book				
UK	0.50	0.75	1.15	0.85
Europe	1.00	1.50	2.30	1.70
North America	2.00	3.00	4.60	3.40
Rest of World	2.50	3.75	5.75	4.25

PLEASE SEND CHEQUE, POSTAL ORDER (STERLING ONLY), EUROCHEQUE, OR INTERNATIONAL MONEY ORDER (PLEASE CIRCLE METHOD OF PAYMENT YOU WISH TO USE)
MAKE PAYABLE TO: STRATUS HOLDINGS plc

Cost of book(s): _____ Example: 3 x books at £6.99 each: £20.97

Cost of order: _____ Example: £2.00 (Delivery to UK address)

Additional cost per book: _____ Example: 3 x £0.50: £1.50

Order total including postage: _____ Example: £24.47

Please tick currency you wish to use and add total amount of order:

☐ £ (Sterling)　☐ $ (US)　☐ $ (CAN)　☐ € (EUROS)

VISA, MASTERCARD, SWITCH, AMEX, SOLO, JCB:

☐☐☐☐☐☐☐☐☐☐☐☐☐☐☐☐☐☐☐

Issue number (Switch only):

☐☐☐

Start Date:　☐☐/☐☐　　Expiry Date:　☐☐/☐☐

Signature: _____

NAME: _____

ADDRESS: _____

_____

POSTCODE: _____

Please allow 28 days for delivery.

Prices subject to change without notice.
Please tick box if you do not wish to receive any additional information. ☐

House of Stratus publishes many other titles in this genre; please check our website (**www.houseofstratus.com**) for more details.